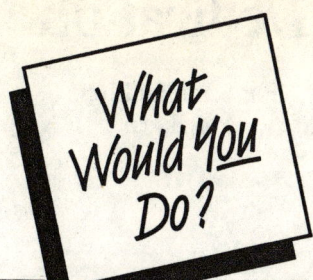

Just This Once

By Dean Feldmeyer

Group

Loveland, Colorado

Dedication

For Sarah and Ben.
My kids.

Just This Once
Copyright © 1990 by Dean Feldmeyer

First Printing

All rights reserved. No part of this book may be reproduced in any manner whatsoever without written permission from the publisher, except in the case of brief quotations embodied in critical articles and reviews. For information write Permissions, Teenage Books, Box 481, Loveland, CO 80539.

Credits
Edited by Eugene C. Roehlkepartain
Cover and Book Designed by Judy Atwood Bienick
Cover and illustrations by Rand Kruback

Scripture quotations are from the Good News Bible in Today's English Version. Copyright © American Bible Society 1966, 1971, 1976.

Library of Congress Cataloging-in-Publication Data
Feldmeyer, Dean, 1951-
  Just this once / by Dean Feldmeyer.
    p. cm. — (What would you do? : 2)
  Summary: The reader makes choices that shape this story of the consequences of drug and alcohol use, including drunk driving and peer pressure to use drugs.
    ISBN 1-55945-106-8
    1. Plot-your-own stories. [1. Drug abuse—Fiction.
2. Alcoholism—Fiction. 3. Christian life—Fiction. 4. Plot-your-own-stories.]
I. Title. II. Series.
PZ7.F33578Ju 1990
[Fic]—dc20   90-34282
                                                                                 CIP
                                                                                   AC

Printed in the United States of America

Introduction

Wouldn't it be nice if the Bible just said, "Thus saith the Lord: Don't drink alcohol and don't do drugs"? No more questions, no more doubts, no decisions to make. Just a law—plain and simple.

Alas, it's not that way.

Of course, there's Isaiah 5:11: "You are doomed! You get up early in the morning to start drinking, and you spend long evenings getting drunk." But the verse seems more concerned with drunkenness than with drinking itself.

Then there's Proverbs 23:31-32: "Don't let wine tempt you ... The next morning you will feel as if you had been bitten by a poisonous snake." That seems like a fairly straightforward warning.

But the Psalmist sings praises of "wine to make him happy" (Psalm 104:15). And Paul tells Timothy, "Do not drink water only, but take a little wine to help your digestion, since you are sick so often" (1 Timothy 5:23).

Why can't it be easy? It would help if the Bible said, "Just say no."

But it doesn't. So in the end, we're left to our own discretion, judgment and responsibility. We have to decide.

Just This Once is a book about decisions and consequences. It's fiction—the characters and the events aren't true. But they *are* real. The decisions and consequences you'll read are the same ones you and thousands of other young people face every day.

How will you decide? What will you do? This book asks those questions. You'll make the choices that shape the story. And consequences will follow. Then you'll have to make other choices.

Here's how it works: Start reading the book at the beginning. Then when you reach a decision point, choose how you want the story to continue, and turn to the page that's indicated. The choices you make will determine the story.

I hope you'll read the book several times. Make different choices and see what happens. Try alternate paths, and see where they lead. If you make a mistake—a bad decision—while reading the book, it won't hurt you. You can always go back and try again.

But if you make a mistake out there ...

Just This Once

David Pearce had never felt better. He'd beaten Darrel Swams.

Darrel Swams! Mr. Darrel All-City-Offensive-Guard Swams.

Put his helmet right in the guy's numbers, drove with his legs and laid him on the ground.

Once Swams was on the ground, David had a clear shot at the quarterback. So he tackled him. No, sacked him for a 10-yard loss.

That play gave the Tecumseh High School Warriors the ball. And they let the clock tick down the final seconds. They were headed for state semifinals for the first time in 26 years ... thanks to a tackle by none other than Mr. David Pearce—the game's undisputed star.

As he sat in his mom's Mustang, outside the Knights of Columbus Hall, David let the scene from earlier that day run through his mind in slow motion—just like an instant replay on television. He imagined the color-commentator lauding the skill displayed in that tackle.

It seemed almost ironic that he—Mr. Clean-Cut Christian—was the school hero today. His youth leader had warned him about the pressures he'd feel to compromise his beliefs if he got into sports. But he'd resisted the pressures. And the guys on the team respected him for it. His pastor had even congratulated him after the game. And his folks were so pleased they let him use Mom's prized Mustang. He had it made!

"Great tackle, Dave."

"Hey, thanks!" David responded, startled from his daydream. He didn't really know the guy. Someone from school. John something.

"You coming in? Sounds like things are rockin' and rollin'."

"Yeah." David could hear the heavy, bass beat of the rock music thumping in the Knights of Columbus Hall across the parking lot. "Yeah, I'll be in."

"Gonna be some celebration!" the guy said. "See ya, inside."

David checked his hair in the rearview mirror. He peeled the small Band-Aid from the bridge of his nose. The bleeding had

6 JUST THIS ONCE

stopped. But he put on a fresh Band-Aid anyway. A small badge of courage that showed how hard he'd hit Swams.

He snapped his collar outside his crew-neck sweater and was ready to go. As he unfolded his long legs from the Mustang, he heard a high-pitched laugh from across the parking lot. He stopped to see who it was.

"Hey, Davey! My man!" came a voice out of the darkness.

David squinted and took a step toward the familiar voice.

"A toast to our friend and leader," David heard another voice announce. "Gentlemen, I give you Mr. David Pearce."

Now he recognized the group. They were guys from the team. From what he could tell, they were passing around a wine bottle.

The ringleader was Drake Underwood, David's closest friend. As he got closer, he recognized some other guys from the team.

"Hey, you gonna stand there with your mouth hangin' open? Or you gonna come join the party?" Drake yelled.

David could still hear the music pounding in the dance hall. He glanced toward the door where several couples had gathered in the cool, night air.

David wasn't sure he should go over to the guys. They were obviously drinking, and he knew they'd pressure him to join in the "celebrating." Drake had a reputation in youth group for being a little too wild. But David also knew how stuck-up he'd look if he didn't go over. After all, these guys were the ones who won the game with him.

"Well?" said one of the guys. "Come on!"

What would you do?

If he goes over to the guys, turn to page 66.
If he goes in to the dance, turn to page 35.

"Well," David said, glancing at the keg. "A small one, I guess."

"Great! Rita?" The Pence persisted.

"Half a glass for me, Warren."

Warren winked at her. "Yeah. Designated driver, huh?"

He was back in a flash with two big plastic cups overflowing with cold beer. "They only come in extra-large," he said, grinning.

They thanked Warren and walked around in the yard and the house, accepting congratulations and sly winks. Rita found a phone in the kitchen and called to tell her dad not to pick her up at the dance; David Pearce, the football hero, would bring her home.

David and Rita held hands, sipped their beers and walked some more. Soon their glasses were empty. Magically, Warren was at their side with new, full cups. They thanked him and sipped a little more.

David tried to remember what he'd read about body weight and blood alcohol levels. But he couldn't recall. Two beers in an hour probably wouldn't be a problem, though.

By the end of the second beer, David began feeling the alcohol's effect. He was beginning to loosen up, laugh a little louder and feel less awkward in the big crowd of people, most of whom he didn't know. But he figured he was still in control.

The beer had obviously affected Rita. Through the evening, she'd gradually gotten closer and closer to him. By now, she was giggling and whispering to him. She wanted to leave.

She—Rita—wanted to leave with him! It seemed too good to be true. So David promptly swallowed the last of his beer, got his car keys and led her to the Mustang.

The late hour ensured that the roads were fairly empty. When David dropped his hand from the gear shift, her hand was there to meet it. He glanced at her, and she gave him a shy smile. The radio played mellow rock, and November air drifted through the car.

"What a great night," Rita said when the radio went to a commercial. "My dad's so excited he can't see straight. He was on the team that went to state semifinals 25 years ago."

"Really?" David replied, genuinely interested. "What position?"

"Oh, I dunno. He told me, but I don't think we use the name anymore."

"Split end?"

"Yeah, that's it. Anyway, he says they had a really big blowout celebration back then. Beer and a bonfire and everything." She paused, as if remembering her dad telling the story. "Some of the guys got caught breaking curfew and almost got suspended from the team."

David laughed. "A team curfew? Are you kidding?"

Rita laughed too. "No, really! They had to be in by, like, 10 p.m."

"Shees! Our whole team would be suspended."

They laughed and talked as they drove around, enjoying each other's company. David drove slowly through town checking out all the hot spots where kids gathered. Bruno's Pizza. Home Boy's Pancake House. The Surf. They were all hopping with celebrating kids.

"David?" Something was different about Rita's voice. Softer, lower. He took his eyes off the road for a split second to look at her.

"Yeah?" He could hardly see her in the shadow.

"You ever ...?"

"Ever what?"

"This."

He glanced at her again, and this time he saw. She was holding a joint between two fingers, like a cigarette. He tried to hide his surprise. "Pot?" he asked.

Rita shrugged her shoulders. "Yeah. I don't usually do drugs or anything. But this girl I know had these at the dance, and she gave me one. And I thought, well, you know ..."

Rita paused, perhaps hoping David would say something. When he didn't, she continued. "It's a special night. My friend said it's great. You want a ... hit?"

A hit? David was shocked. Hadn't she noticed his reluctance to drink at the party? Surely she knew he was a Christian. On the other hand, maybe she'd never talk to him again if he turned her down. And he'd heard marijuana wasn't addictive—at least some people said that.

What would you do?

If he consents, turn to page 121.
If he refuses, turn to page 56.

JUST THIS ONCE 9

10 JUST THIS ONCE

The little white pill did it for David. The verbal abuse hurt his feelings. But he could take it. The drinking was disgusting. But he had tolerated it.

But the pill was too much. And now Drake was trying to rationalize his drug abuse by acting as if everyone did it.

Well, baloney! Everyone didn't do it. And Drake could take his wine and beer and little white pills and go straight to some alley if he thought David would stand around passively and be insulted for saying what he believed.

For what seemed like a long time, David stared at Drake, sitting in the car with that vacant smile on his face. Finally, he turned to walk away.

"Hey!" Drake called after him. "Don't go away mad."

David turned and glared back. "Drake ... you are one sick puppy."

As he walked across the parking lot he thought he heard Drake giggling, but he wasn't sure. And he didn't look back to check.

He'd gotten away from Drake, and he'd stood up for what he believed. But David wasn't sure what to do next. He cared about his friend, and he figured Drake needed some help. On the other hand, he had his own problems. And if Drake wanted to mess up his own life, maybe that was his business.

What would you do?

If David decides to talk to someone about Drake, turn to page 11. If he tries to forget Drake and take care of himself, turn to page 14.

Monday morning, David couldn't keep his mind on English literature. He kept thinking about Drake sitting there in his car, tapping out a rhythm, smiling vacantly.

The idiot was sick—so sick he didn't even know it. That was the worst part. He really thought he was okay.

David guessed the drugs did that to a person's mind. Drugs and alcohol. Why couldn't he make Drake see that?

Every time he tried to talk to Drake, David felt like he was swimming upstream in a strong river—in over his head and getting sucked deeper with each stroke. Maybe he should talk to someone. But who?

Coach Clark? No way! Coach was a great guy, but he was a stickler for rules. He'd suspend Drake from the team. And that would only make things worse. Besides, telling Coach would make David a snitch. No way!

His parents? Maybe. But they were already uptight about drugs. One word about Drake's problem, and his parents would forbid him to see Drake again. And they might even call Drake's parents. David couldn't imagine the problems that would cause.

Jeff Marsh? Now there was a possibility. David couldn't bring himself to think of his pastor as Rev. Marsh. The guy was too easy to talk with to be a "Reverend." Besides, he preferred to be called Jeff. And didn't ministers have something that kept them from telling things people told them? Confidentiality or something like that.

But even as good as he was, Jeff was still an adult. No matter how private their conversation, David would feel he was betraying Drake. He wasn't sure why. He could talk about it without using names.

Maybe he'd try one more time to talk to Drake. Maybe. But he was getting harder and harder to talk to. Especially when he was high or drunk—which was more and more often.

What would you do?
If he talks to his pastor, turn to page 51.
If he tries to talk to Drake, turn to page 70.

12 JUST THIS ONCE

David couldn't believe what he was hearing. "Drake, I'm your friend."

"Friends accept each other, man!"

"You're not making sense!" David said, reaching out for Drake's arm.

Drake pulled away violently, opened his car door and leaned on it. "You're so ... so ... " He paused, looking for the right word. "Straight! You're so ... uptight! You oughta be 30 years old."

"Because I don't drink or do drugs?" David could feel his neck getting hot with anger.

"No, because you're so stupid!"

"Stupid?"

Out of his pocket, Drake pulled a tiny white pill, popped it in his mouth and swallowed it. "Yeah, man. Stupid. Wake up! It's everywhere!"

"Everywhere?"

"Athletes, rock stars, actors, politicians, cops. Nobody stays straight anymore. You gotta get high to get by." He sank into the car and began beating a rhythm on the steering wheel. "Lighten up, my man! Get with the program. It's the '90s."

David felt numb. Was he out of touch? Was Drake right? On the other hand, he'd just heard kids say they wanted to stay away from drugs and booze. Maybe Drake was the one who was out of touch.

What would you do?

If David tries to talk more to Drake, turn to page 10.
If David considers that Drake may be right, turn to page 16.

"Just say no," he said to himself. But it seemed hollow. Unreal.

There was no "just" to it. It's hard being different. Being straight. Especially when everyone else seemed so bent.

He caught himself again. Everyone?

No! Not everyone! In fact, not nearly everyone. Probably not even half the people he knew did drugs. And probably 20 to 30 percent of the kids in the school had never touched alcohol—much less gotten drunk.

So it wasn't everyone. It was some people. Some. A *few*. But that didn't mean he should. Besides, some people rob banks or run around naked in the snow. Just because people do stupid things didn't mean *he* should.

So there it was. It didn't matter if everyone else in the whole country was doped up all the time. David Pearce wouldn't do drugs. And he wouldn't drink alcohol. Because it was dangerous. Stupid. And he believed God wanted him to take care of his body.

His friends would have to learn to accept him for who he is.

Blind choice:
Without looking ahead, turn to page 41 or page 79 to see how David's friends react to his decision.

14 JUST THIS ONCE

All day Monday, David tried to put Drake, drugs and alcohol out of his mind. Forget him, he told himself. You've got enough to worry about without him. Midterm exams, calculus, the state semi-finals, new football plays.

It worked ... sort of. But it was like when he was worried about asking a girl out and he couldn't concentrate. His dad would say, "Well, think about something else." And it made him think about the date even more.

That's the way it was with Drake. Every time he thought he'd put Drake's problem out of his thoughts, the image of that little white pill would float through his mind.

Finally, mercifully, classes ended. Now football practice would begin, and he could put himself into something he could do something about.

No sooner had he sat down in front of his locker and begun to untie his shoes than it began.

"Woof! Woof!"

"Here, boy! Fetch, boy!"

Laughter erupted around him, but he didn't know what everyone was laughing about. Had he missed something?

"Here, Drake!" someone called out. "Fetch, Drake."

It was Bert Roberts, one of Drake's drinking buddies. Now tailback Tom Fisher joined him. "Hey! Stop callin' ol' Drake. He ain't gonna fetch."

Brian Donnenworth, the big defensive end, stuck his head around the lockers. "What? Drake ain't gonna fetch? Will he roll over? play dead?"

Tom sat down heavily on the bench and shook his head. "Nope," he said. "Can't do anything like that."

"Why not, Tommy?" asked Bert, too seriously, David noticed. They must be reciting lines.

"Because he's sick," Tom said, shamelessly overacting.

"Drake, sick?"

"Yeah. I guess we could say he's ..." Tom started giggling almost uncontrollably. He held his side as the giggling turned into gales of laughter. "He's one ... sick ... puppy!"

Now everyone was standing around David laughing uproariously as Drake burst out of David's locker, a dog biscuit in his mouth. He took a bite of it, chewed and swallowed, smacking his lips. The other three guys collapsed in laughter.

JUST THIS ONCE 15

David couldn't help himself. He smiled. Drake looked so ridiculous, standing there in his football pants, munching contentedly on a dog biscuit. "M-m-m," Drake was saying. "Liver and bone meal. My personal favorite." He reached into David's locker and pulled out a box of the biscuits and thrust them at David. "Want one?"

David reached hesitantly into the box and took one out. Slowly, he put it to his mouth.

"O-o-o-oh," the others moaned.

"No, man."

"This is too gross."

"You two are crazy!"

Drake put his arm around David's shoulders. "This is more like it. No hard feelings about this weekend?"

David shook his head.

"Great!" Drake said, giving the others high-fives. "Hey, look, guys! My man is smiling. Check it out! You don't see it often. Fun ain't at the top of his priority list. This is truly a beautiful moment!"

David couldn't say anything. He just shook his head and put his dog biscuit back into the box. This was the old Drake—fun, sober, cutting up, crazy. If only he could be like this all the time.

Drake was talking again. "... teach this man how to have fun after we win Saturday. He's forgotten how to enjoy himself. But fear not! Dr. Drake has the perfect remedy." He leered at David and headed for his own locker.

And in that leer, David thought he saw a little white pill pass, like a ghost, between himself and Drake—an unwelcome reminder of the dangerous remedy Drake would recommend.

As he put on his pads, David tried to decide what to do. Maybe Drake was right. Maybe he was too stuffy. But he also knew how messed up Drake was when he was high or drunk. Maybe, David thought, he should talk to someone about it.

What would you do?
If David considers that Drake may be right, turn to page 16.
If David decides to talk to talk to someone, turn to page 51.

Was he wrong about people using drugs? Was Drake right?

Well, no, of course not. Not everyone did drugs. He knew lots of people who didn't do drugs. Drake's self-justification was ridiculous.

But what about the other stuff Drake said?

Was David too straight? too stiff? Did he act more like an adult than a teenager?

Life had seemed pretty serious lately, with the big game and midterms and all. Maybe he was taking it all too seriously—cutting people off, turning them away without even realizing it.

That night at home, he pulled his Bible off the bedstand from underneath his football playbook. Mr. Becker, his Sunday school teacher, had been encouraging class members to read Romans on their own time.

That's as good a place as any to start looking for guidance, David decided. As he paged through the thin pages, he came across Romans 3:20: "For no one is put right in God's sight by doing what the Law requires; what the Law does is to make man know that he has sinned."

David knew "the Law" in the passage referred to the Old Testament laws, but he figured, in this case, the verse might apply to laws about drug use.

He kept flipping pages and came across Romans 6:1-11. He highlighted verses 6 and 7: "And we know that our old being has been put to death with Christ on his cross, in order that the power of the sinful self might be destroyed, so that we should no longer be the slaves of sin. For when a person dies, he is set free from the power of sin." Did that mean Christ had the power to help people overcome addictions?

By now, David was engrossed. He read most of chapters 7 and 8, then skipped over to chapter 12. He'd always wondered about verse 2. What did it mean to "not conform yourselves to the standards of this world"? How does God transform you "by a complete change of your mind"? Heavy stuff.

He thought he had a clear-cut answer to his dilemma when he read verse 9: "Hate what is evil, hold on to what is good." That indicated he shouldn't give Drake a second thought now.

Then he read Romans 14:12: "Every one of us, then, will have to give an account of himself to God."

David closed his Bible. It wasn't his place to judge Drake.

JUST THIS ONCE 17

But he did need to make a decision for himself. He tried to decide what to do. Should he continue to completely avoid alcohol and drugs? Or should he relax his standard so he can fit in better?

What would you do?
If David decides to stick with his standard, turn to page 13.
If David decides to relax his standard, turn to page 67.

18 JUST THIS ONCE

The cars, according to the police, had been traveling faster than 50 mph on the expressway three miles out of town. One of the cars—a van, actually—had been carrying a family of five.

The van was totaled. The doctors in the emergency room said the family had been lucky. Had they been in a car, they all would've been killed.

As it was, the mother was still in critical condition. The father had multiple head, leg and internal injuries. One kid, a 3-year-old girl, had a broken collar bone and was being held for observation. The other two, both 8-year-old boys, had been treated for cuts and bruises and released.

The other car had been an old, green Oldsmobile with gray primer over the rust spots. The police knew this much because someone told them. They couldn't have figured it out from the wreck. There wasn't enough of it left.

The driver was dead. He'd been completely drunk. One cop said you could smell the booze from inside of what was left of the car. The liquor was why the driver had been going the wrong way on the expressway.

The driver's name? The cop flipped through some papers on his clipboard. Since the next of kin had been notified, he'd said, "That name would be ... Underwood. Drake Underwood."

■

David retold what happened about like that—like he was testifying ... Just the facts. Sammy Wu, John Metzger, Rachael Thomas, Trent Dressler and Bobby Themes listened without interrupting.

There wasn't much to say. They'd known Drake was dead for almost 24 hours. Hearing David tell it as he had gotten it that night from the police and Drake's parents was like filling in the blanks.

The silence was heavy and cold as they sat around the table in the school lunch room. None of them felt like eating—though they'd all bought or brought lunches. John sighed. Rachael held his hand. Bobby ate a couple of green beans, chewing slowly, deliberately.

"So ... What now?" Sammy asked, without her usual enthusiasm.

No one answered. But they all knew. The grief. The funeral,

JUST THIS ONCE 19

with everyone from school there. Even kids who didn't know Drake would come. It was a reason for getting out of class.

Nothing new. It had happened before. And it would happen again.

Rachael had overheard her parents saying how they were always surprised when they didn't see in a Saturday newspaper that some kids had been killed in a car wreck. Such things were almost commonplace.

All the teenagers there wished they could do something to get people to stop drinking and driving. They'd talked about forming a SADD chapter—Students Against Driving Drunk. But they'd never really done anything. And now Drake, someone from their own church, was another victim. Could they really do any good? Or were they just kidding themselves?

David felt the pain the deepest. After all, Drake had been his best friend. What would he encourage the group to do now?

"What do you think, David?" Bobby finally asked.

What would you do?

If David urges the group to organize a SADD chapter, turn to page 113.
If he tells them to give up, turn to page 119.

20 JUST THIS ONCE

The silence was endless. David realized he was holding his breath and started breathing again, quietly. Sammy shuffled in her chair.

Drake stood up. He hooked his thumbs in his jean pockets and then laughed. He tilted his head back and laughed loud and long. But it didn't sound like laughing. David wasn't sure what it sounded like. And it ended as quickly and surprisingly as it had started.

"You all make me sick!" Drake screamed. "You're so righteous and perfect. You make me sick! You think I need you? You really think I need any of you? Well, I don't! I don't need anybody. I can take care of myself!"

And he stormed out.

Mr. Underwood started after his son, but Dr. Frieze stopped him. "No! Let him go. Maybe he'll change his mind. Give him time."

"But, he's my son! Where will he go? He'll die out there on his own."

"He'll die anyway, Mr. Underwood. The alcohol's slowly killing him. But worse, Drake's drinking is killing your family—you, your wife, your marriage. Give him time. He may change his mind."

"He'll get drunk," David protested. "I could tell by his eyes."

"Yeah, the whole time we were talking to him, all he was thinking about was how bad he wanted a drink," Rachael said.

One by one, people put on their coats. Before they started out, Jeff Marsh stopped them.

"I realize you're all feeling a lot of things right now," he began. "That's okay. There's one thing you need to remember: Whatever Drake does tonight, you didn't cause it. If he gets drunk again, it'll be nothing new. He was going to get drunk anyway. Only now you won't be helping him do it. You aren't going to lie for him or make excuses for him or hide his alcoholism anymore."

He paused in thought. "For the first time, Drake is going to have to take responsibility for his own drinking."

Everyone sat in silence as the statement sunk in.

"Before we leave," the pastor added, "let's pray together. For Drake ... and for his friends and family." They joined hands.

"Dear God, we're frightened, confused and worried for our friend Drake. Protect him, God, and help him understand he doesn't have to live life trapped by a bottle or a pill. Help us, Lord, to continue loving Drake with a love that insists he take responsibility for his own actions. Amen."

David left the meeting alone and walked home through the darkness. What would happen to Drake now? Had David done the right thing? Whatever happened, he knew things would never be the same.

Blind choice:
Without looking ahead, turn to page 18 or page 97 to learn what happens to David and Drake.

22   JUST THIS ONCE

"Oh ... What the heck!" David heard himself say. Instantaneous cheers arose when David went over, took the bottle and swallowed a small swig of the cheap, bitter wine.

"Davo! I knew you'd come through," Drake drawled. "See, guys! He can knock 'em down on the field and knock 'em down his throat!"

That was just the first of many bad one-liners from the drinking football players. David tried to laugh, but he was more worried than amused. He hung around to listen to the drunken banter for a while. Then he headed home, excusing himself because of a headache—which he told the guys was from the hit on his head, though it really came from the wine.

■

Surprisingly, Drake appeared at church the next morning. He looked hung over as he sat on one end of the old couch in the youth room, resting his head on his fist, his eyes closed.

As Mr. Becker started the lesson, David couldn't keep his mind from wandering back to the events of the previous day. The game. The parking lot.

"David, what do you think?"

Mr. Becker's voice startled David. His mind quickly came back to the class. What had they been talking about? a parable or something? about seeds?

He felt lost. "I'm sorry, Mr. Becker. My mind's not here today."

"No problem, David. Is there something you'd like to share?"

"Uh ... no. It's nothing."

"Well," Mr. Becker said, "if you change your mind, you'll find we're pretty fertile soil where listening is concerned." He smiled at his own pun.

It must be the parable of the sower after all. Oh, well.

David looked again at Drake, sleeping (or pretending to sleep) in the corner. David hesitated a few seconds, then changed his mind. "Okay," he said, looking around the room. "I do have a concern."

Mr. Becker seemed surprised. Some kids stirred and showed interest.

"Well," David went on. "I've never considered myself a religious person, you know? I mean, I go to church and everything, but I don't think I'm any better than anyone else."

"Aren't those things, in themselves, being 'religious'?" Mr. Becker queried.

"Maybe, I don't know ... But the thing is, I don't drink. Okay? It's no big thing. I just don't."

"And?" Mr. Becker prodded.

"Well ... " David looked at Drake, saw an eye flick open, focus on him and close again. "Well, sometimes it feels like I'm the only person in the whole school who doesn't drink or do drugs.

"I don't think anyone's doing much about it—all the drinking and drugs, I mean," he continued. "We—our church—should be able to do something to tell people what they're doing when they take that stuff."

"Well, I don't do drugs!" said Rachael Thomas.

John Metzger echoed Rachael. "Me neither. I've had a couple of beers before. But I just decided it's all too dangerous."

"Drugs," Trent Dressler added. "You never know what you're getting."

Other kids chimed in:

"You do if you buy from your friends, your bro's!"

"Where did your friends get it?"

"What about the police?"

"Yeah, what about getting arrested?"

The discussion rolled on and couldn't be stopped. Mr. Becker closed his lesson book and tried to direct traffic. Several kids said they didn't do drugs or alcohol. Sometimes they felt pressure. Sometimes they didn't. Sometimes they didn't care. Sometimes they did.

Then, as abruptly as it had started, the discussion ended and class was over. Rachael announced she was going to Home Boy's for a pancake brunch, and several kids went with her. The others filed out to the parking lot to meet their families for dinner.

As he started across the parking lot, David saw Drake standing beside his Olds. Their eyes met, and Drake nodded his head in a "come here" motion. David thought about ignoring it, but decided Drake—now sober—probably felt bad about last night and wanted to apologize.

But he soon realized he was wrong.

"Why don't you get off my back?" Drake snarled, his eyes blazing.

"What? I don't ..."

"That whole thing in there was about me! Don't act so innocent!"

"Drake, I ..."

"You're worse than my old man. If either of you really cared about me you'd accept me the way I am and stop trying to change me."

David was stunned and confused. He didn't know what to say. Drake obviously needed to be straightened out, he thought to himself. But maybe he should keep his mouth shut until the whole thing blew over.

What would you do?

If David decides not to confront Drake, turn to page 12.
If David argues with Drake, turn to page 104.

JUST THIS ONCE   25

"This is your fault, Davo! You just couldn't leave well enough alone, could you?"

"Had to keep stirring things up, didn't you?"

"The storm troopers have descended—thanks to you!"

David didn't know what to say. What were they talking about? He'd driven his mom's car to school early Wednesday morning for a team meeting to watch films of last week's game, and teammates had cornered him in the locker room.

"Everything was cool until you started riding your holy horse."

"What!?" David said, desperately. "What's goin' on?"

No answer. The guys just snorted at him, turned and walked to the meeting room. Trent Dressler, from church, was team student manager. David approached him as he unpacked rolls of tape and stacked them on a shelf in the training room.

"Trent? What's everyone so mad about? What's going on?"

Trent didn't look at him. He continued deliberately stacking the tape.

David persisted. "Are you mad at me too? What'd I do?"

Finally, Trent whirled and slammed the box of tape down on the training table. "I don't do drugs, and I don't drink. Okay? So I've got nothin' to hide. But I still don't like it. Just 'cause we're students doesn't mean we don't have rights."

"What rights? Trent, what's going on? I just got here. I'm lost."

Trent cocked his head skeptically. "You don't know about the searches?"

"What searches?"

"The lockers. Hamner the Hammer heard about you worrying about drugs and stuff. And he called the cops. They're searching all the lockers in the school right now for drugs."

"Can they do that?"

"They're doing it, aren't they?"

"But don't they need a warrant or something?"

"Apparently not. You walk through that locker room door and you give up your privacy."

"Trent, you gotta believe me. This wasn't my idea ... really!" David heard himself pleading, and he didn't like it. But what could he do?

"Yeah, well, that isn't how everyone sees it. Even if you didn't suggest it, you at least gave Hamner the idea."

David wasn't sure what to do—or think. Trent turned around

26 JUST THIS ONCE

to continue his work, and David sat on a bench to think through his options. In a way, he was glad someone was doing something. The student council hadn't seemed too enthusiastic.

But he also felt the vice principal's action was a little dramatic. It didn't seem to fit what he'd learned in government class about privacy and individual rights.

He knew he had to decide. He was on the firing line now. He couldn't stay neutral.

What would you do?
If David supports the searches, turn to page 32.
If he decides to confront the vice principal, turn to page 91.

On Monday night, David played a hunch and drove by Bruno's Pizza. There she was, sitting by herself at a booth by the window, reading.

"I feel like I owe you an apology," he said, standing awkwardly by her table.

Either she hadn't seen him or she was a good actress—the surprise in her eyes seemed genuine. "Oh, hi, David." She seemed nervous, didn't know what to say next. "Uh, what are you doing here?"

"I saw you through the window. I came to apologize."

"For what?"

"Come on, Rita. Don't make it any harder for me, okay?"

She closed her book and laid it on the seat beside her. Her expression softened. "You wanna sit down? I guess we oughta talk, huh?"

He guessed they oughta. So he sat, and they talked. About lots of things, but mostly about drugs and drinking and their relationship.

"Rita, I feel like we really got off on the wrong foot. I mean, I really like you, and I ..."

"What happened?" she asked.

"I dunno, I guess it all seemed to move so fast ... The party ... The car ride ... Everything, you know," he responded.

"I know what you mean, David. What're we going to do now?"

He didn't want to make her feel any more uncomfortable than she already was. "I guess I've been a little too tight in the past. I mean, one glass of beer won't kill me."

"I agree," she said, looking up. "But drugs are illegal and dangerous anyway. Doing pot and pills and stuff is pretty stupid, I guess."

"Yeah, drugs aren't for me. But you can be responsible with alcohol. I mean, my parents say the difference between a social drinker and a drunk is responsibility."

She smiled at him. It melted his heart. "Just because you're responsible doesn't mean you can't have fun," she said, winking.

She smiled and took his hand in hers. Things would be okay, David thought as he relaxed. "Want some pizza or something?" she asked.

28 JUST THIS ONCE

■

That Saturday, Tecumseh High beat Middleston by less than a touchdown to take the state semifinal. Next week they'd play Plainsville for state. David didn't shine, but he played well.

To celebrate the victory, Warren "The Pencer" Pence threw another party. David and Rita had a perfect chance to practice responsible drinking.

But responsible drinking was easier to plan than do—especially when The Pencer was constantly shoving full cups of beer into their hands.

At first, David just felt good. The victory, the fatigue from playing the game, being with Rita, lots of congratulations from the kids all combined for a natural high. The beer just made it all go down smoothly.

Three beers and he was talking freely about key plays in the game. He'd put his normal inhibitions behind him and was boasting freely. And he loved the attention it brought him.

Five beers and he was drawing diagrams on the snack table, using pretzels as football players. Rita had drifted off somewhere, but he didn't care. He was having a great time.

Somewhere around 10 beers he lost count. Who cared? This was a party. He deserved the chance to let his hair down—celebrate a little.

Around midnight, he started feeling a little dizzy.

At 1 a.m., he got sick and barely made it to the bathroom.

At 9:00 the next morning, he woke up in his own bed without the slightest idea how he got there. His head hurt. His stomach was rolling like a ship in a storm. His mouth tasted like he'd cleaned the bottom of his shoes with his tongue. And the smell of bacon wafting up from the kitchen sent him racing for the bathroom where he spent 20 minutes sitting in front of the commode wishing he could die.

Shees! he thought. What have I done? I let it get out of hand. I gotta get control! Rita! What happened to her? How did I get home? I'd better call.

But his head hurt so badly that the thought of talking on the phone sent him back to the commode.

His mother called up the stairs. Did he want breakfast?

"No, just some juice, Mom," he called back to her, knowing

from her voice that she knew why he was sick.

He hoped he'd be able to keep that down.

His condition made him nervous. Being responsible wasn't as easy as it seemed. Maybe he needed to talk to someone about it—like his parents. They were "responsible drinkers." On the other hand, this was just the first time. He'd learned his lesson. Next time he'd probably be able to handle it.

What would *you* do?
If David decides he can handle it, turn to page 46.
If he decides to talk to his parents, turn to page 60.

30 JUST THIS ONCE

"Davey, my man. Where are you?" Drake screamed over the phone. It was after midnight, and he was wide awake.

"I'm home," David said. "Drake, I need your advice."

"Women or booze?" He laughed loudly. Was he drinking again?

"Women," he said. "That is, one woman."

"Would this woman be a certain, tall, beautiful, dark-haired, brainy cheerleader whose initials stand for Rita Marley?"

"Well, yeah. How'd you ... "

"I saw you leave the dance together. The Draker has eyes everywhere." He laughed again. "Spill your guts. Women are my specialty."

So David told him. Not the details, of course. But he gave him the general picture. It felt good just talking about it.

There was a long silence over the phone, and he wondered if Drake was still listening. If he was drinking he might have fallen asleep.

"Drake? You still there?" he said, finally.

Then, screaming again, Drake said, "David Pearce. This is my advice: *Get your gnarly butt over here right now!*" He hung up. Well, that clinched it. Drake was drunk. "Gnarly butt" was a phrase he only used when he was drinking. And then he used it constantly.

David didn't know how much help Drake would be to him drunk. But Drake usually wasn't a "bad" drunk. And he was someone to talk to.

So he went.

■

"What you need is a little hair of the dog," said Drake holding up a bottle of vodka. David didn't recognize it. "Russian," Drake said. "The best!"

"I don't know, Drake. I just ... "

"Drink! Then talk!" Drake wooed. "A little oil to lubricate the vocal chords." He handed David a large glass. "Vodka and 7-Up. Pure nectar."

David took the glass reluctantly. He hadn't come here to drink. He'd come to talk. But it looked like talking would be impossible without at least pretending to drink Drake's vodka. He took a sip.

JUST THIS ONCE 31

Not bad. No burn, like he expected. Sweet, with just a hint of alcohol.

Drake was reading his mind. "Smooth, huh? My old man would never buy a vodka that burns. Only the finest for him. Heck of a guy, huh?"

"Heck of a guy," David agreed. He drained the glass and held it out for another. Might as well join the party, he thought. Drink first, talk later.

But he didn't do much talking. Drake talked non-stop all night. And, it seemed to David, he got funnier and funnier as the alcohol took effect.

And with each drink the worries, the problems with Rita—all the problems, for that matter—just slipped away. Without even talking about them, they were gone. And Drake was asleep on the waterbed, snoring loudly.

Well, time to go.

David nearly fell down the outside stairs, but caught himself on the third step from the top by grabbing the railing. Whoa, he thought. Maybe a few too many. Have to be careful. Especially driving home. Don't want any trouble in Mom's Mustang. Have to take it re-e-e-e-al easy.

Blind choice:
Without looking ahead, turn to page 76, page 120 or page 126 to learn what happens.

32 JUST THIS ONCE

By lunch, David knew what he had to do.

"Look, I don't like locker searches any more than anyone," David explained, taking a bite of his burger. "I've got personal stuff in my locker."

"Tell me about it!" Samantha Wu said, dipping three french fries in ketchup. "I keep a fresh outfit in my locker—underwear and all! I was humiliated." She was a cute, smart sophomore with a goofy personality. Everyone called her Sammy.

"You keep underwear in your locker?" asked John Metzger, taking a seat at the table. "Can I see?" He winked at David.

"Why not?" Sammy said. "Everyone else has."

David stole one of John's fries. "Oh, Sammy, they didn't hang it from the flagpole. They just looked under it and put it back."

"That's not the point, David," Rachael Thomas said. "It was personal stuff, and they had no right. We have a right to privacy."

"All I have in my locker is books and dust balls," John said, smiling. "They're welcome to look." He was teasing Rachael. Everyone in school (except Rachael) knew he had a thing for her.

She didn't like the teasing. "You guys aren't taking this seriously. We don't give up our constitutional rights when we come to school."

"Whoa! Constitutional! Did you just learn that word?" John said, winking at David again. "Five syllables!"

"The point is," said David. "The war on drugs is just that—a war. We have to take drastic measures to win. We all have to make sacrifices."

Sammy threw her hamburger on her tray, let her shoulders sag and stared open-mouthed at David. "David! Whose side are you on?"

"I'm with anyone who wants to get rid of drugs and alcohol."

"So locker searches are okay?"

"If that's what it takes."

"What about body searches? Are those okay too? We're all guilty until proven innocent. Is that it?"

"Look, Sammy, I don't have all the answers." David sipped diet Coke while he thought. "I just think we have to set aside some rights to win this thing."

Sammy and Rachael looked at each other, stood up and walked away.

"Ouch!" John said. "Kinda intense, huh?"

Why can't anything be clear-cut, black and white, David wondered as he finished his lunch in silence. His friends had some good points. But he also believed strongly that something had to be done. Maybe he should talk to the vice principal about the raids. Or maybe he should ask his parents how to deal with the situation.

What would you do?
If David shares his concerns with the vice principal, turn to page 91.
If David shares his concerns with his family, turn to page 123.

34 JUST THIS ONCE

It took a lot of effort to forget about Rita. Suddenly, it seemed like he saw her everywhere—at school, at the mall. And every time he saw her for several weeks, he'd have to swallow hard to keep his composure.

Making matters worse, he'd heard the rumors Rita was now spreading about him. About how he's a square prude. "You can have more fun on a date with a worn-out mannequin than with David Pearce," he overheard her say during lunch when he was sitting by himself at a nearby table.

But the more he thought about his choice and the more he watched Rita, the more he realized he'd made a good decision. Rita might be beautiful and fun to be around, but her values and priorities were so different from his that they'd always be fighting if they were together.

Besides, no one—including Rita—was worth messing up his body for. And no one was worth compromising his beliefs.

Sure, it was hard to stand up for what he thought was right. But what about the alternatives? Destroying his body with drugs or alcohol? Hurting his witness as a Christian? Some things were more important than making everyone like you.

David decided it didn't matter if everyone in the whole country was doped up all the time. He wouldn't do drugs.

His friends would have to learn to accept him for who he was.

Blind choice:
Without looking ahead, turn to page 41 or page 79 to see how David's friends react to his decision.

JUST THIS ONCE

The Knights of Columbus Hall was hot, loud and crowded when David walked in. But no one seemed to mind. The disc jockey was spinning a mixture of Top 40. As David meandered toward the refreshment table, guys slapped his back, shook his hand, told him how great he was. Girls flirted with him.

It was heady stuff. And he loved it.

Then, suddenly, there she was, standing right in front of him. Rita Marley. Tall, thin, athletic, with long, black hair that fell just below her shoulders. Great smile. Smartest girl in the class. Cheerleader. Student council member. The list seemed endless.

She and David had been sneaking looks at each other, talking between classes and kidding around for about a week now. But he hadn't worked up the courage to ask her out.

"Congratulations, David," she said, smiling. What a smile! And she didn't call him Dave or Davey—both of which he hated.

"Uh, thanks." Great. Good return. Idiot! He tried his boyish grin. If he couldn't talk, at least he could smile.

"I heard Swams was the best," she said, giving him another chance.

"He was tough. Kept me out of some key plays. But Coach showed me some tricks. I guess I got lucky." Oh, that was awful. He sounded like a dumb jock. Here he was an honor student, and he couldn't even carry on a conversation with a pretty girl.

Then, as though the DJ read David's mind, a slow-dance song filled the hall, and couples covered the dance floor.

David nodded toward the other couples. "Wanna dance?"

Rita was good at dancing too. None of that stand-in-one-place-and-sway-back-and-forth stuff. Real dancing! She made it seem easy—and made him look good too. And she could almost look him in the eye, which at his 6-foot height was rare.

One dance faded into another and another. And the next thing he knew, David had taken off his sweater and was rockin' with Rita. They danced and talked and danced some more and drank Cokes and danced some more.

Finally, as the dance began to wind down, Rita asked David if he wanted to go to a party she'd heard about. He did and he didn't. He wanted the night to go on forever, and the party could at least add a couple of hours.

On the other hand, he'd also heard about some of the post-game parties at people's houses. If he thought the pressure to drink was bad in the parking lot, the party pressure would be twice as bad. And a bottle of cheap wine wouldn't be the only problem. Beer, liquor, weed, crack—anything was possible.

But he figured he could handle the pressure. After all, he handled Darrell Swams on the football field. He put his arm around Rita and said, "Sure, let's go."

■

Before they could see the house, David and Rita saw the cars. And if the number of cars was any indication, this was one totally successful bash.

And it didn't take long to see why it was so successful—beer.

People were drinking everywhere. In the yard, in cars, in lawn chairs on the patio and, it seemed, in every room of the house. The host, Warren Pence, was running around frantically trying to please all the guests.

His dad was dispensing beer from a huge keg on the patio. "There you go," he'd say, handing someone else a brew.

David was trying to figure out how Mr. Pence could draw the beer so accurately—always with a half-inch of foam. Then Warren bumped into David. "Hey, Dave! Great game! Great tackle!" He pumped David's hand. "Great party, huh?" He looked around the patio. "We may have to make another beer run."

"Pretty great, Pencer. Lotta people," David said, looking around. He wondered how many would've come if the keg had been filled with diet Coke.

"Yeah." He paused. "Hey, what'cha drinking? We got beer or beer."

"Oh, well, uh, I'm in training..."

"Ah, come on. One won't hurt you. We're goin' to state semis!"

David looked at Rita and raised his eyebrows. What do you think? Rita shrugged her shoulders and tilted her head non-committally. Not much help.

What would you do?
If David accepts a beer, turn to page 7.
If he turns down the beer, turn to page 99.

JUST THIS ONCE 37

38 JUST THIS ONCE

David was sitting in Jeff Marsh's messy study again. Same chair. Same mess on the desk. He'd asked Jeff what to do, and Jeff had suggested they force Drake to confront his problem head on.

David wasn't comfortable with the idea. "It sounds ... I don't know ... sneaky, I guess. Like we're tricking him or something," he said.

"It is sneaky," the minister said.

"Yeah," David said. "So?"

"David, we used to think the only way an addict could get clean was to hit bottom. But we say that in quotes now." Jeff lifted both his hands and drew quotation marks in the air. "Hit bottom."

He leaned back in his chair, and it squeaked loudly. "Now we know we don't have to sit around and watch until addicts are utterly unsalvageable, hoping they'll realize how desperate their situation is. Before they get that far, we can create a bottom for them to hit."

"Create a bottom?" David thought he understood, but he wasn't sure.

"Yeah. It's called an intervention. We call together his friends and relatives—everyone who cares about him—and we sit him down and do three things." He stuck up fingers as he talked. Jeff was great for lists. He constantly used them in his sermons.

"First, we tell him how his drinking makes us feel, and we give him specific times we've felt that way. Second, we tell him, specifically, what we want him to do about his drinking. And third, we tell him what we'll do if he doesn't."

David was trying to put it together. "And then?"

"And then, either he agrees to our demands or he doesn't. If he does, maybe he'll get well. If he doesn't, we do what we said. The consequences have to be severe enough that he won't want them to happen."

David watched Jeff lean back in his squeaky chair and smooth his mustache. "You mean, like, if his parents say they'll throw him out if he doesn't stop drinking, and he doesn't stop, they have to throw him out?"

"Right."

"But what if he ..."

"He's already dying. Eventually the alcohol and drugs will kill him. And right now it's killing his family and friends too. What we're saying to him is, 'Look, Drake, we don't want you to kill yourself with booze. And we don't want you to hurt us with it either. We want you to stop drinking and we're willing to help. We hope you'll accept our help. But accept it or not, we're not going to be hurt by it anymore.' "

"It seems so ... selfish," David said.

"In a way, yes. We're taking care of ourselves for a change. Drake is invited to take care of himself too. It's also the best way for Drake—the only way he'll deal with his problem. But it's his decision."

"I dunno." David shook his head. "Isn't there a nicer way?"

Jeff shook his head. Not to say no, just to sympathize. "Yeah, David. There's another way. We can go on making excuses for him and lying for him. And while we're at it, we can pick out a headstone and buy a plot over at Shady Grove. Because that's where we'll be sending him. We do those things, and he'll just keep drinking."

"I know," David said, looking at his hands folded in his lap. After several minutes of silence, David finally said, "Okay, you win. We'll do it your way."

"Let's hope everyone wins, buddy," Jeff said. He pulled a yellow legal pad out of a pile on his desk and laid it in his lap. "First, we make a list of everyone who cares about him and is aware of his drinking."

David smiled. "Well, just about everyone at school knows. I don't know how many care anymore."

They wrote the list. Some they could call on the phone. Others they'd have to visit. Jeff would talk to Eric Frieze, a psychologist from Eastside Clinic—someone who was qualified to lead the intervention. Everyone would meet on Friday evening to discuss the plan. Then, on Sunday night, they'd spring the trap. Those were David's words: "Spring the trap."

Jeff smiled at him. "It's not easy, David. God knows I know that. Do me a favor?"

David nodded. "Sure."

"Let's get this thing started on the right foot, okay? Let's ask for God's help." Jeff bowed his head and spoke quietly: "Lord, we love Drake, and we're worrying about him and hurting for him. Help us translate our worry and hurt into something that can help. Give us words and feelings adequate for the task, so we can bring one of your children back to you."

It wasn't easy getting everyone there—Drake's parents, David's parents, other friends, Coach Clark. But they managed. The hardest part was Drake. Finally, they decided David would go pick Drake up and say he wanted to talk about some stuff.

The plan worked. Drake was clean, sober and reasonably well-rested when he walked into the room. Shock, surprise, wonder, doubt, worry and anxiety all flashed across his face when he saw his friends, parents and coach seated in a circle in the middle of the youth room.

"Drake, I'm Dr. Frieze from Eastside Clinic. I asked your friends to call these folks here tonight. They have some things they'd like to tell you."

And the intervention began. First, people in the circle each told Drake about a time when his drinking had hurt or embarrassed them. They told about what they saw alcohol doing to him.

Then they told him what they wanted him to do. Enter the clinic. Tonight. Go with Dr. Frieze and start getting well.

If he didn't? That was the hard part. They would drop him. No invitations. No friends. No lying to protect him. No making excuses for him. He would have to move out of his home. He would be on his own.

They didn't stop there. One by one, each person said: "I love you, Drake. I want you to be well. I won't watch you kill yourself with alcohol."

Then it was over. It was up to Drake now. Dr. Frieze had said this would be the hardest part—wanting so desperately to go to him, to hug him, and not being able to do it. They had to let him—make him—make his own decision to be well.

David wiped a tear from his eye. Why didn't Drake say something? Why did he just sit there with his head down and his elbows on his knees?

Finally, Drake raised his head and looked around the room.

Blind choice:

Without looking ahead, turn to page 20 or page 88 to discover Drake's reaction.

"I'll have a diet, thanks," David said.

Drake reached deep into the cooler, wincing as the ice numbed his hand and wrist. "Uh huh, uh huh," he said, feeling around under the surface. Finally, his hand popped out holding a can of diet Coke. "This do?"

"That'll be fine," David said. He popped the top, and they toasted.

A bunch of guys had gotten together for a friendly spring baseball game. Drake was drinking beer, of course. But Drake didn't say anything about David's choice. No one did anymore.

At first, back in football season, it hadn't been that way. There had been some teasing and, a couple of times, out-and-out insults. But they hadn't lasted long. His friends—his real friends—had stayed beside him.

For a while David thought of his choice as a witness—a role model. He'd live a life clean and free of drugs and alcohol. He'd show that it could be done, should be done. He took 1 Corinthians 6:19-20 as his motto: "Don't you know that your body is the temple of the Holy Spirit, who lives in you and who was given to you by God? You do not belong to yourselves but to God; he bought you for a price. So use your bodies for God's glory."

But if it was a witness, it seemed like a mute one. In five months, he hadn't seen any change in his friends. They drank. They occasionally did drugs. It was as though being drug-free was just another insignificant option in their lives—like whether to order fries or onion rings.

At least they hadn't gotten worse. That was the problem with this kind of witness. He never knew what a person *didn't* do because of his influence. He never knew what kinds of temptations they'd overcome.

And, David thought, he probably never would. That was between them and God. He just kept on being himself. And he hoped God would use his choice to his advantage. Sometimes that was all he could do.

"... a friend of Drake's?" the voice beside him said.

David turned to see a guy who was about his height, maybe an inch taller. Broad shoulders, thin waist, light brown hair and deep-set brown eyes. He might've been handsome if he wasn't so ... so big. His arms strained the sleeves of his T-shirt.

"Yeah. I've known him since fourth grade," he replied.

The guy just nodded his head and looked over David's shoulder, obviously trying to think of something to say. David decided to help.

"I'm David Pearce," he said, extending his hand.

"Rich Martin," the guy said, taking David's hand. David was surprised at how weak the shake was. "D'you go to Tecumseh?" Rich asked.

"Yeah, I graduate next month."

"M-m. I go to Monroe."

"I didn't think I'd seen you before."

"Oh, I've seen you," Rich said. "I play tackle. Offense and defense."

David nodded and smiled. Now he remembered what Rich looked like in football gear.

"I've seen you at parties. You don't drink," Rich said.

"No." David had learned that one word was all the explanation needed.

Another pause. "Drake says you're straight," Rich commented.

"Does he?" David said, a little uncomfortably. "Well, Drake and I are friends. But we differ on drinking."

"You're in pretty good shape," Rich said.

"I work out." David wondered if this guy always carried on such weird conversations—bouncing from one subject to another.

Rich blew out a long breath. He turned to David and looked straight at him. "You ever take anything ... you know ... to make you stronger?"

"Nope."

Rich nodded. "I figured ... He said you were straight."

David decided he'd have to push to get this conversation going. "Look, Rich," he began. "Is there something ... "

"I gotta get off it, man," Rich blurted out. "I'm scared. I'm scared it's gonna screw me up some way ... if it hasn't already."

Now David saw it. How could he have been so blind? The muscles, bigger than any 17-year-old should have. The nervousness. The questions.

"Steroids?" he asked, taking a sip of his diet Coke.

Rich nodded. "They're messing me up, man. I can feel it." Rich's intensity was almost frightening. "I thought, just a couple, you know. To help me get started. This guy I knew at the gym, he said he could ... "

David held up his hand. "Rich. I know someone who can help. He's my minister. But he's cool. And he knows some people who offer treatment. I'll introduce you if you want."

Relief flooded into Rich's face. David felt it too. It works, he thought. It really works. What I do—my witness—really can make a difference.

The End

David decided he couldn't let a little teasing keep him from doing something about the drug problem he saw in the school. He asked a couple of friends from church to help him, and he put up fliers all over school.

"FIGHT DRUGS AND DRINKING AT TECUMSEH HIGH. Meet in the student council room at 3:30 p.m. on Thursday to decide how to make a difference."

Only six other students came—mostly David's friends. Rita Marley. Trent Dressler, the football team's student manager. Rachael Thomas. John Metzger. Bobby Themes. And Samantha Wu, who everyone called Sammy.

When everyone settled down, they all looked at David. "Hey, I just thought we should talk about it. I didn't say anything about being the leader," he said, holding up his hands.

"Looks like you're elected," Bobby said.

"Okay," Sammy said. "Now, what's next?"

"Well," David replied, "I dunno, really ... I guess we educate people."

"About what?" Trent asked.

"About advanced calculus." Rita quipped. "What do you think? We educate people about drinking and stuff."

"How do we educate?" John asked. It was the first time David had heard him be serious about the subject.

David cleared his throat. "Our pastor knows a guy in Monroe who started a SADD chapter. He's getting us some stuff."

"That's all well and good," Bobby said, "but don't we need to deal with more than drunk driving?"

"It would be nice," David added, "but maybe this is a good way to start. The program works in other schools."

"Great!" Bobby agreed. "Then I move we adjourn until we see what your minister got."

They decided to meet at Bruno's for pizza at 6:30 on Monday. Rachael said she'd invite Rev. Marsh.

■

The beginning was that simple. The group turned out to be as enthusiastic as it was small.

Jeff Marsh brought a whole shopping bag full of posters, brochures and fliers. Their first order of business, they decided, would be the "Contract for Life." It wasn't a radical agenda, but it could actually save lives and give the teenagers something tangible to do.

In the contract, signed by teenagers and parents, teenagers agreed not to drive if they'd been drinking. Neither would they ride with a driver who'd been drinking.

In return, parents agreed to provide transportation home for their teenager—regardless of the hour—if their kid drank or didn't have a sober driver to ride with. They also agreed to not fight or talk about the situation at that time, though they would expect to talk about it later.

Parents also agreed that they would not drive drunk or ride with a drunk driver.

■

That night, David's parents signed and dated the contract. "I think this is a good idea, David," his dad said. "You understand, though, that it doesn't mean we approve of you drinking alcohol."

"Sure, Dad," David answered. "I don't like the idea of you getting drunk either. This way everyone can sleep easier."

"Yeah. I guess so." He folded the contract and put it in his jacket pocket. "So, you got, what, a dozen kids in this group?"

"Six ... so far."

"That's not many."

"It's a beginning ... somewhere to start."

Mr. Pearce nodded his head, picked up his coffee and headed for his recliner in the family room. "I just wish there was an ending."

So did David. He hoped his group would find one. But could he really change anything? He wouldn't know until he tried. Isn't that what his dad had always told him?

So he would try.

As he climbed into bed that night, David pulled out his Bible. He'd been neglecting devotions lately, he realized. The bookmark was in 1 Corinthians 10. As he read the passage, his thoughts settled on verse 31: "Well, whatever you do, whether you eat or drink, do it all for God's glory."

He prayed that his efforts would fit that verse.

Blind choice:

Without looking ahead, turn to page 81 or page 137 to continue the story.

46 JUST THIS ONCE

When his parents confronted him about his drinking, David snapped, "Mind your own business, and I'll mind mine." He was in control, he figured. He just needed to find out how much he could hold.

He had plenty of chances to do just that. There was always a party to go to. Someone to hang out with. But somehow he never managed to stop drinking when he "reached his limit."

■

One Saturday night after a party, he was driving home when flashing blue lights and a siren pulled him over. David was angry. Incensed. Indignant. And a little drunk.

"Aw, give me a break. No way I'm drunk," he said, trying to sound reasonable, after the cop questioned him and gave him a Breathalyzer test.

"No, sir," the cop said, not looking up. "You're not drunk—not according to the laws of this state anyway."

"So, what's the problem, officer?" Finally, the guy was being reasonable.

"No problem, sir. You just sign here. I've called a cab to take you home." He extended the ticket pad to David.

"Sign? Sign what?" The pad blurred a little before his eyes.

"Sign the citation, Mr. Pearce. You're not admitting to anything. Just saying you received it."

"But why?" The indignation came back in his voice. "You just said I'm not drunk."

"How old are you, Mr. Pearce?"

"Eighteen."

"Your mother's maiden name?"

"Uh ... Regis. What's my mother's ... "

"How many beers d'you have?"

"Uh ... five ... six ... I dunno. Not many. But I'm *not* drunk. I could feel them sneaking up on me, so I quit and headed home. I'm not ... "

"No, sir, you aren't drunk. You are, however, under the influence of alcohol. And you're underage. And you were driving."

"Aw, give me a break!"

"I am. I should take you in. But I'm letting you go home in a cab. Just show up in court on the day on the ticket with one of your parents."

"One of my parents?"

"Yes, sir. Here's your cab. You got any money?"

David nodded. He couldn't speak. His mouth had gone completely dry. One of his parents. Oh, no! What would he do? What would his parents do?

Blind choice:
Without looking ahead, turn to page 74 or page 109 to see how David's parents respond.

JUST THIS ONCE

David couldn't bring himself to take Drake in. He felt like he'd be betraying his best friend. Everywhere he looked, it seemed, people were rationalizing drug use. If not their own, then other people's.

"It's my body," they'd tell him. "I can abuse it any way I choose." This was usually accompanied by a laugh, because they didn't believe they were abusing their bodies with drugs. "No harm. I don't see any victims here. D'you see any victims?"

Maybe there was a little truth in some of the stuff they said. Life really was tough for some kids. Half the kids he knew came from broken homes. Many had at least one alcoholic in the family. There never seemed to be enough money in his own family—and both of his parents worked. What must it be like with only one parent to feed everyone.

Some kids had parents that didn't pay any attention to them. Bert Roberts, the tight end, was all-conference. And his parents had never been to a game.

Maybe some of the kids were right. Maybe he was too harsh, too judgmental about drugs. Maybe if he was in their shoes, he'd be doing drugs too. Perhaps he should lighten up some.

But if you lighten up, isn't that the same as saying it's okay? "Yeah, I know, your life is hard. No problem. Go ahead and take a hit. I'll turn my head while you fry your lungs and brain."

Well life was hard for everyone. No one had been singled out for a tough adolescence. Drugs, sex, sports, grades, girls, parents, siblings, friends, college, jobs. It was all tough. And drugs only made it tougher.

At least that's what he thought.

He didn't know, though. He didn't do drugs. And he didn't drink. But should he force his beliefs on everyone?

What would you do?

If David decides to lighten up, turn to page 67.
If David decides to organize an anti-drug group at school, turn to page 44.

Suddenly David sat up on the blanket, breathing heavily. A fine sheen of perspiration covered Rita's face, and she wiped it away with her sleeve.

David took a deep breath and let it out slowly.

"I ... I just can't," he finally breathed.

Rita stood abruptly and walked to the car.

She's mad, David thought as he heard the door open and close. She thinks I don't like her.

But before he could complete the thought, she was back, sitting on the blanket. She handed him a diet Coke. It was warm now, but it gave him something to do.

The silence seemed to go on and on as he drank his warm soda and looked at the dark, quiet river. Finally, Rita broke the silence. "I really meant what I said."

"H-m-m-m?"

"What I said, David ... I really do love you. I have ever since I first saw you. I knew we should be together."

"Yeah ... great," David said nervously. "I think you're great too."

She leaned against his arm and took his hand in hers. Her voice was still different. Not quite slurred, but lazy. Husky. Foggy. Sexy.

The weed, he thought. It makes her voice like that. What else does it do? Does she really love me? Or is it the weed talking?

He hoped it wasn't the weed. He hoped it was the way she felt—when she wasn't high.

He hoped it because he felt it too. He thought he might be in love with her. She did something to him. Just thinking about her made his pulse quicken. Her smile. Her touch. Her voice. Everything about her turned him on.

Everything but the weed. And as long as the weed was there it was like a wall between them. He couldn't bring himself to return her love.

"Maybe we'd better go," he said. It sounded so empty.

He felt Rita sag against him. She sighed again. Then she said, "Yeah, okay." She stood and walked to the car.

Neither of them said anything on the way home. When they got to Rita's house, he didn't offer to walk her to the door. He didn't know why, he just couldn't. It made him feel awful.

"Good night," he said, as she got out of the car.

50 JUST THIS ONCE

"Yeah," she said.

As he drove away, David felt like he'd ruined any chance he ever had of dating Rita. What would she say to him now? Should he try to forget her? Or should he try to make up?

Blind choice:
If he decides to forget her, turn to page 34.
If he tries to make up, turn to page 27.

"The thing is, he was so hung over in Sunday school he could hardly keep his eyes open." David was pacing back and forth in the pastor's office. "He drinks constantly. And now he's taking pills to get over the hangover."

He sat down abruptly, suddenly self-conscious about his pacing.

Pastor Jeff Marsh had curly hair, a thick black mustache and reading glasses. His office was in a constant state of confusion. He leaned back in his chair and laced his fingers behind his head.

"What kind of pills is he taking?" he asked.

"I dunno. He didn't say."

"You saw the pill?"

David nodded.

"What color was it? How big?"

David considered. "It was white ... And real little."

Jeff considered a moment, then nodded. "Speed," he said.

David raised his eyebrows in a question.

Jeff leaned forward and put his hands together on top of his desk. "It's not uncommon for someone who drinks to take speed. It speeds up the heart and masks the symptoms of hangovers—headache, nausea, lethargy. It gives you energy."

"Is speed addictive?" David asked.

Jeff shook his head. "Well, it may not be physically addictive. But psychologically it is. See, Drake drinks to calm down. Then he gets hung over and can't get cranked up again. So he takes some speed, which winds him up. Then he needs something to wind down again. So he drinks again."

David's shoulders slumped. "Shees, it's a cycle."

Jeff shrugged. "Yep."

"Can he break it?"

"Sure, but he'd have to go cold turkey. He'd have to drop both of them at once. It would be rough for a couple of weeks."

"Weeks?"

"Yeah. Speed is absorbed into the system then released a little at a time. Without the alcohol, he'd get constant rushes. He'd have trouble sleeping and would crave something to make him relax."

"Can you help?" David asked.

Jeff shook his head. "Drake's out of my league, David."

"But I thought you were a drug counselor or something."

"I volunteered in a drug clinic back in seminary. Mostly, I mopped up after the junkies. We need to get Drake into the drug rehabilitation clinic."

"I dunno. The clinic. I've heard some stuff ... "

"It's no picnic. But I know a guy who works there. Why don't we go talk to him?"

"Jeff, I already feel like I've betrayed Drake's confidence by talking to you. Wouldn't that be like narcing on him? I mean, talking behind his back and all?" David realized he was standing and pacing back and forth again.

Jeff considered for a moment then said, "Yeah. You'll have to talk behind his back. And, in a sense you'll be betraying his confidence."

David looked at him, disbelieving. He'd expected Jeff to brush this excuse off and try to talk him into it.

"But what if Drake told you he was going to shoot himself in the head?" Jeff continued. "Wouldn't you betray that confidence?"

"This is different," David said.

Jeff stood up and began putting on his jacket. "No, not really," he said. "Drake's going to kill himself on drugs and alcohol if he isn't stopped."

David looked at him then. "You think?"

"I know. I've seen it."

David shook his head and rubbed his temples. Suddenly his head hurt. "I don't know," he said. It seemed like such a radical thing to do—putting Drake in a clinic. Maybe he could talk some sense into Drake without betraying his confidence anymore.

What would you do?

If David decides to talk to Drake about his problem, turn to page 70.

If he agrees to visit the clinic with his pastor, turn to page 54.

JUST THIS ONCE 53

▼

Monday morning, immediately after homeroom, David raced to the stairs just outside the library. Rita had to pass by to get to her second-period class.

When he saw her, she was talking with Barb Miller, carrying her books close to her chest like all the girls did. And she was wearing the navy-blue sweater he liked so much.

He timed it so he'd start up the steps just as Rita and Barb did. "Hi, Rita," he said, smiling.

"Oh, hi, David," she said.

And that was it. She turned back to Barb and continued talking.

Something similar happened outside the lunch room. And again after school by the parking lot. By the end of the day, David felt uncomfortable just seeing her.

It was clear she didn't want anything to do with him. He wasn't cool enough for her. He'd blown it. He wanted to cry. He wanted to hit something. Somebody. He wanted to hide somewhere and not come out.

That evening as he worked on his English term paper, David wondered if he should just forget about Rita. On the other hand, he really liked her. It might be worth trying again with her.

What would you do?
If he decides to forget about Rita, turn to page 34.
If he tries to make up with Rita, turn to page 27.

54 JUST THIS ONCE

"We have to remember that alcoholism is a disease," explained Dr. Eric Frieze as he opened his office door at the Eastside Clinic.

The psychologist, David and Jeff sat down in the sparse office, and Dr. Frieze poured himself a cup of coffee from the coffeemaker on the filing cabinet. He had classic psychologist looks, David thought—black beard, pipe and tweed jacket with elbow patches.

Dr. Frieze winced at the taste of his coffee and continued talking. "As a disease, alcoholism has three main characteristics. First, it's chronic. Once you have it, you always have it. You want a cup of coffee?"

David shook his head. Jeff got up and got his own.

"Where was I?" Frieze asked. "Oh, yeah, chronic. Secondly, it's progressive. If an alcoholic keeps drinking, the alcoholism will get worse. And third ..." He held up three fingers. "... it's fatal. If the alcoholic keeps drinking, it will eventually kill him or her."

Jeff was wandering around the office, looking out the window. "How does an alcoholic quit?" he asked, more for David's benefit than for his own.

Dr. Frieze shrugged. "Depends. About 10 percent just quit—that's it."

The rest? The other 90 percent? David wondered.

"The rest have to have help," Frieze said.

"But Drake can be cured, right?" David asked, hopefully.

Frieze shook his head. "Never cured. But he can be sober, if he wants."

"How?"

Now Jeff came over and sat down.

"From what you tell me," Dr. Frieze said, holding his coffee mug with both hands. "Drake should be admitted to the clinic immediately."

"Immediately?"

"Today, if possible. It'll take about three days to let the alcohol drain completely out of his system. Another five or 10 for the pills. Those days'll be rough. He may experience panic, anxiety, even D.T.'s."

David looked to Jeff for an explanation.

"Delirium, hallucinations," Jeff said. "Part of withdrawal."

"Shees," David said, shaking his head. He thought it was just a little drinking problem. Nothing this serious. How did it get so out of hand?

"No visitors for five days," Dr. Frieze was saying.

"Not even you. After the worst is over, he'll be allowed a few visitors. His family, his pastor, you. Then he'll need your support and love."

He tasted his coffee, made a face and set the cup on his desk. "For now, though, it's between him and the bottle."

"What if he won't come?" David asked.

"Put your friendship on the line," Frieze said matter-of-factly. "Tell him to come in, or you won't be there for him."

"Risk my friendship?" It sounded so ... drastic.

"If he was standing on a window ledge 50 stories up, would you risk your friendship to get him back into the building?"

David didn't answer. He didn't know what to do.

What would you do?
If David agrees to get Drake to the clinic, turn to page 58.
If David refuses to bring Drake in, turn to page 48.

"I don't do drugs, Rita," he said, staring straight at the road.

"Yeah, me neither. But I thought..."

"I *don't* do drugs," he snapped.

"*Okay!* You don't need to get mad."

David sighed, tried to relax. "I'm not mad. I just ... it's just ... they scare me. All drugs do is blur your thinking and distort reality."

"Yeah, reality's so great," Rita said sarcastically.

"It is for me. I like reality fine." And why shouldn't he? He'd made a great tackle to win the game. He was out with his dream girl. That stuff was real. Dream girl! Oh, Lord, he hoped he wasn't blowing it.

"... just weed," she was saying.

He took a breath. Why stop now? "Besides that, Rita, even if the other stuff isn't true. What about the smoke? The smoke in a joint is as hot as a furnace when it hits your lungs. It burns lung tissue you breathe with. It clogs up those air sacks ... I forgot what they're called."

"David ..."

"I work hard to keep my body healthy. I go to practice. I work out. And my mind too. I work hard in school so I can handle reality, not run away from it." There. He'd said it. He wondered how she'd respond.

"Are you through?" she asked.

"Yeah, I guess so," he said. She wasn't handling it well, he could tell.

"David, I've been wanting to go out with you for a long time, okay?"

"Really?"

"Everyone said, 'He's too uptight.' But I didn't listen to them ..."

"Who said that?"

"That's not important. The point is, I just thought they didn't know you well enough. I knew you'd be fun once I got under that serious exterior."

"Rita, I ..."

"I mean, you're cute and everything. How could such a cute, talented guy be such an old man? David, lighten up. Laugh a little. Life's too short."

"Do I really come off that serious?" he asked, a little shocked.

JUST THIS ONCE 57

"Do people really say that stuff about me?"

"Guilty on both counts," she said.

"Shees!" he exclaimed. "I didn't know."

Rita shrugged her shoulders.

"Rita," he said, trying to explain. "My parents have always taught me your greatest investment is in yourself."

He glanced into his rearview mirror, looking for the right words. "The thing is, I've made a big investment in myself—all the work I do and everything. So if I sometimes come off too serious, that's why. I just don't want to screw up my investment ... Does that make sense?"

Rita shrugged. "I guess so ... Yeah, I guess it kinda does."

They drove in awkward silence for several minutes. Finally, he drove her home. She said, thanks, she had had a great time. But it didn't sound sincere. It hadn't gone exactly the way he'd hoped.

That Sunday, after church, he called her.

"Hello?"

"Hi, Mrs. Marley?"

"Yes?"

"Uh, this is David Pearce, Rita's friend. Can I speak with Rita?"

"Oh, hi, David. Uh, Rita's not ... she's not here right now. May I take a message?"

Not there? At noon on Sunday? Right!

"No, that's all right. I'll call back later, thanks."

"Okay. Bye, David."

He hung up without saying goodbye. He guessed he'd blown it. Had he come off too strong? too serious? Was she mad at him? He wished he knew.

Blind choice:

Without looking ahead, turn to page 53 or page 27 to continue the story.

58   JUST THIS ONCE

"David had some doubts that you'd come in," said Dr. Frieze, smiling.

Drake shrugged his shoulders and forced a smile. They sat down in the psychologist's office. He was hiding his nervousness well. Only his shaking knee gave him away.

The tour had been positive and upbeat. David was still a little awed by the Eastside Clinic. It was nothing like the snake pit that rumor held it to be. The youth wing was clean and fairly new. The only thing that revealed its age was the smell of stale cigarettes.

David had called ahead to tell Dr. Frieze they were coming. Johanna met them at the door. She was tall, maybe 17, with a pretty smile. She was friendly—even bubbly.

"You must be Drake," she'd said, extending her hand toward him and ignoring David. "I'm Johanna. I'm an alcoholic."

Drake shook her hand indifferently. "Yeah," was all he said.

"We're going to meet Dr. Frieze in the dining hall," she said. And she was off, with David and Drake scurrying to keep up.

They had seen the whole place: the dining hall, the recreation room, the solarium and the rooms. Johanna accompanied the tour with an endless commentary about how much she'd drunk and what kind of drugs she'd used.

Finally, Dr. Frieze told her she could go work on her other duties. "Sometimes she gets a little carried away," he told Drake after she left. "But she means well. She's been sober for two years now. She comes in and does volunteer work twice a week."

The tour was over and the moment of truth had come. Dr. Frieze explained the "soberization process" as he called it. "How bad do you want it, Drake? How bad do you want to be sober?"

Drake met his gaze. "The worst," he said, quietly.

"I can call your folks to tell them you've checked in."

"What about the cost?" Drake asked.

"That's between me and your folks. Your only worry is getting straight." He waited a moment. "Okay?"

Drake took a deep breath and let it out. "Call 'em," he said.

Blind choice:
Without looking ahead, turn to page 96 or page 107 to discover if the treatment works for Drake.

▼

Sunday, David called Rita after church. But her mom said she wasn't home. When would she be back? Well, her mom wasn't sure ... Later.

She was obviously covering for her daughter. But he waited and called again after a couple of hours.

"Oh, hi," Rita said. It wasn't an enthusiastic greeting, and he felt something like guilt creeping across his shoulders.

"I was wondering," he said. "Could we, uh, talk?"

"Go ahead," she said.

"Well, I meant, like face to face."

"Oh ... uh ... I've got a lot of homework, and my parents don't want me to run around on Sunday. It's supposed to be a family day, you know, and they like having me around so we can do family stuff."

It was too much explanation. She could've said the same thing with half as many words. So it was probably something else.

"Rita, please? I feel like ... I dunno ... like we should talk. Can we get together?"

"Maybe Monday," she replied.

Blind choice:

Without looking ahead, turn to page 27 or page 53 to see how Rita will respond.

"Look, when I was 16 I got my license. I had good enough judgment to handle a car. How is this different?" David was sitting on the edge of the couch, his arms resting on his knees.

Mr. Pearce folded his newspaper with a sigh and tossed it on the coffee table. "Well," he said. "First of all, driving is legal when you're 16. Drinking isn't."

"That doesn't make sense."

"It doesn't matter. It's the law."

"Then you agree it doesn't make sense?" David asked smugly.

"I didn't say that," his father shot back. "Alcohol is tricky. You have to be able to make judgments—responsible judgments—while under its influence."

Mrs. Pearce hadn't said much to this point, but she tried to enter the conversation. "You see, David. You have to be able to say: Whoa! I'm getting a little tight here. I'd better stop."

"Tight?" This was a new one to David.

"High," his father said. "Same thing."

He looked to his dad. "Can you do that?"

"I don't get tight. I just have a drink now and then. A social drink ... when we go out or when I want to relax."

"Then you don't just drink it. You use it," David said triumphantly.

Then, as if his father was reading his mind, Mr. Pearce said: "Look David, this isn't some kind of game. It's not a debate where you score points against me, then you win the debate, and I say it's okay for you to drink. It's not okay. I really don't want to discuss it any further." He picked up the newspaper and started to unfold it again.

David could feel the anger building in his chest and throat. He hated it when his father did that. He stood and walked toward the kitchen. "You know what that makes you, don't you?" he asked, turning back to his parents.

Mr. Pearce looked at him as if to say, are you still here?

David gave the look right back. "Hypocrites." He looked at his mother. "Both of you." Then as he walked into the kitchen, "Do as I say, not as I do."

His father shot back, "Whatever you call us, we're still your parents. And until I'm convinced you're responsible, I'm taking away your car keys."

JUST THIS ONCE **61**

JUST THIS ONCE

■

David was rummaging through the cabinets looking for the Oreos, slamming things around when his mother came in. As she pulled out a kitchen chair and sat down he could hear her sniffing.

Why did she always have to cry? He hadn't meant for it to get so personal, to hurt her feelings. It was supposed to be a discussion. He found the Oreos and took a handful. But he couldn't bring himself to turn and look at her. He ate them while looking out the window.

"You got the last word," she said, finally.

"Mm."

"You remember your Uncle Mark? We used to go out to his farm and ride his horses when you were little. Your feet wouldn't reach the stirrups so he fixed up a special saddle for you. Remember?"

David turned to her and leaned against the counter, but he couldn't say anything. Mark had been his favorite uncle. Always fun and funny and full of energy. Mark had been killed in an automobile accident five years ago. Driven his jeep into a tree way out in the middle of the farm. His wife and kids had found him late that night when he didn't come home for supper.

Mrs. Pearce took a napkin from the table and wiped her eyes. "He was drunk, David. That's why he drove into that tree. Your Uncle Mark—my little brother—was an alcoholic."

"No, he just ..."

"Drank beer. I know. That's what we thought at first. But it's true. Aunt Ginny told us. Do you see, now, why we're so concerned?"

David didn't know what to think. He was angry and confused. How could his mom say that about Uncle Mark? Could it be true? What should he do now?

What would you do?

If he doesn't listen to his parents, turn to page 142.
If he decides not to drink, turn to page 116.

"He lies. He steals—from his own family. Last week we came home, and he'd carried off the television and stereo." Drake's mom broke down again, crying. David sat awkwardly on the couch and watched her.

He'd done everything he could think of. For a while, he'd even thought it was working. He and Drake had cleaned all the bottles and pills out of Drake's room and out of the old cabin Drake called his fort. They'd camped out for a whole weekend, drinking diet Coke, eating, talking until all hours. They even read the Bible together on Sunday morning, since they missed church.

Drake had terrible mood swings that weekend. Giddy one minute; depressed—almost suicidal—the next. And then, late Sunday afternoon, a change came over him.

The experts had been wrong, David had concluded. It hadn't taken weeks to get Drake's system clean. Only three days.

Drake's eyes seemed clear. His voice was controlled. He laughed and talked easily. David could hardly believe it. Could it be this simple?

Later, David would look back on that weekend and wonder at the self-control it must have taken for Drake to pull off such a charade. And worse, he'd pulled it off for two weeks—playing football, doing his homework. And, all the time, drinking and popping pills without anyone knowing.

Now, no one had seen him for two days. David had gone to Drake's house to see if his parents knew where he was.

"We haven't seen Drake for more than a week, David," Mrs. Underwood had said through the screen door.

"A week? I don't understand. I mean, he was in school ... "

"Drake and his dad had an argument—about Drake's drinking. Jim said if Drake didn't stop drinking, he could find somewhere else to live. He stormed out, and we haven't seen him."

That's when the crying started. She backed away from the door, and David took it as an invitation. They sat on the couches, and she told him about her experience with Drake.

Drake had never stopped drinking. If anything, the drinking had gotten worse after that weekend. He didn't even bother trying to hide it from his parents anymore. (Only his friends, David thought.) And he was taking pills too. Every time she saw him, he was popping pills like they were candy.

And lying. Big, bald-face lies. He'd tell his parents he was going to David's house to study. Then he wouldn't come home until the next day after football practice, when he'd apologize and ask them to take him back.

Then the money disappeared. Mrs. Underwood always kept her extra household money (she called it pin money) in her dresser. No one knew it was there. Not even her husband.

Drake had taken it. He must've gone through every drawer to find it. "More than $200," she said. "What could he need all that money for?"

David said he didn't know. But he did. Obviously Drake was moving on to bigger and better highs. Crack probably. Or worse.

Well, after the money incident had come the fight. And that was the last they'd seen of Drake. Obviously, he'd found someplace to stay (to crash more likely, David thought), because he'd gone to school a few more days. But then he'd stopped showing up at school too.

David thanked Mrs. Underwood, said he was sorry about Drake and eased himself out the door. She was still crying when he left, blaming herself. What had she done wrong? They never should have thrown Drake out. Why hadn't she been more observant? a better mother?

A better friend, David thought.

Well, next time would be different. Next time he'd carry Drake over to the Eastside Clinic and chain him to a bed if he had to.

■

But the next time never came.

David didn't see Drake again for four months. Neither did anyone from church or school. Occasionally he'd hear rumors. Drake had joined the Hell's Angels. Or he'd gotten straight, lied about his age and joined the Marines.

But no one had seen him. After a while no one seemed to care anymore. Drake was just a memory—another kid whacked out on drugs. Another runaway.

When David did see Drake in early March, he didn't recognize him at first. He'd lost at least half of his body weight. His hair was long and dirty. And he was filthy.

David would've passed by and not even noticed him if there hadn't been such a big crowd standing around the slide in the playground David passed on his way to school.

JUST THIS ONCE 65

He walked over to see what the commotion was all about and heard some younger kids talking to each other. Drake's name was all he caught, but it was enough. He pushed his way through the crowd and ran into a big cop who caught him by the arm.

"Hey, wait a minute," the cop said.

"I'm sorry," David said, his heart racing. "I thought I heard someone mention a friend of mine ..."

"What? You know this guy?" the cop interrupted.

"What guy?"

The cop shrugged. "Well, if maybe you can identify ..."

"Drake!" David ran to the slide. It took a minute or more to grasp what he saw. When he did, he sank to his knees and wept. "Oh, Drake. Drake."

Sometime after the big snowstorm in February, Drake must've come back to town without anyone recognizing him and piled the snow up around the end of the slide and made sort of an igloo for himself. Not a home, really; just a place to fix.

David knew that's what it was because that was the last thing Drake did. He'd fixed. The needle was still in his half-frozen arm.

"Another OD in the park," the cop was saying. "Fine way to start the week." He helped David to his feet as the ambulance arrived—too late.

We were all too late, David thought.

■

The image of Drake's half-frozen, emaciated body clung to David's mind like a leech. Nothing could make it go away. He couldn't study, he couldn't watch television, he couldn't hold a conversation. He tried to pray, but his thoughts and words were confused and garbled.

He needed to do something. For Drake. For himself. Anything was better than living like this. But he couldn't think. He was too upset. Maybe a sleeping pill would help. Maybe working against drug use would channel his energy constructively.

What would you do?
If David turns to drugs to help deal with his grief, turn to page 110.
If he becomes an advocate against drug use, turn to page 77.

JUST THIS ONCE

Okay, he thought. Why not go see the guys. Just to say hello.

He walked over to where the guys were gathered around Drake's old, beat-up Oldsmobile. Drake was sitting on the hood, leaning against the windshield, a bottle of cheap wine propped against his chest.

"Davey! My ... main ... man!" He slapped the hood of the car with each word. "Was that the greatest tackle you've ever seen or what?"

"Great tackle, man!"

"Unbelievable!"

"Put old Swams on his butt!"

"Thanks, guys," David said.

"Thanks! Thanks!" Drake shouted. "He's thanking us! Can you believe this guy?" He tried to hop lightly from the hood, but stumbled and almost fell, then walked very deliberately toward David. He was drunk.

"No, Davey, dear friend. It is us ... uh ... we who should thank you. Brian! A bottle for my friend!"

"No ... hey, thanks, guys, but none for me," David said, backing away. "I gotta get to the dance." He turned and started toward the door.

"Oh, that's right. I forgot," Drake mocked, leaning back against the Olds. "Mr. Perfect doesn't want to pollute his body. That right, Davey?"

David tried to ignore Drake. He knew it was the wine talking. But the words hit home. He wanted to be included—to be one of the guys. Maybe he was being too uptight. What would a celebratory sip hurt anyway?

What would you do?

If he decides to ignore Drake and go to the dance, turn to page 35.
If he decides to join the guys for a sip, turn to page 22.

David wasn't sure why he'd become so adamant in his standards. Maybe the stress and pressure had caused it. Whatever it was, he decided a little change wouldn't hurt. He'd lighten up; go with the flow. Be more at ease around people and less judgmental.

He'd go ahead and have a drink now and then—just to let people know you could be a Christian, a good student, an athlete and still be one of the guys. Adults—even his parents—did it sometimes, didn't they?

So, after beating Middleston 18 to 14 in the state semifinals, he had a beer at the big blowout party.

It was no big deal. Oh, some kids from church looked at him funny. But no one said anything. And a couple of the guys on the team actually patted him on the back and congratulated him.

"Finally decided to join the human race, huh?" Bert Roberts, the tight end, said.

Tom Fisher, the tailback said, "Brewsky goes down good after a big game, doesn't it, Dave, my man."

And Drake ... well, Drake didn't have to say anything. He just raised his own can in a silent toast and winked at David across the room.

It felt good! Not the beer. He'd just drunk one, and he couldn't even feel the alcohol. No, he felt good knowing he was one of the guys again. Now they knew he didn't consider himself "better" than them.

See, he told himself, you *can* be popular, well-liked and respected—and keep your principles. You just have to be flexible.

■

His choice seemed to make life more simple and fun. The night after the first beer, he had a couple of wine coolers at the school hayride and bonfire.

Then it only made sense to share a six-pack with Drake at the old cabin Drake called his secret fort one weekend when David's parents were gone.

And after dropping the state championship to Newellon by only one touchdown, who could blame him for having a few brews? The alcohol made it not seem so bad.

But maybe he went too far that time. He could still hear his mother's voice echoing in his head when he ate breakfast the next morning.

"David? Are you okay?" she asked.

"Yeah, fine. I just didn't sleep too well ... I'm just tired."

"You look pale. Maybe you should eat. I'll fix bacon and eggs."

The thought of all that grease nearly sent him racing to the bathroom. His head was about to explode, and his stomach was rolling. His mouth felt like it was filled with dust. And why was she talking so loud?

"No! Uh, no, Mom, thanks," he said, excusing himself. "I think I'll just go lie down for a while. Will you call the church and say I can't make it to the clean-up day?"

And, of course, she did.

Shees! That was close. Clearly, he'd drunk too much. He'd have to figure out just exactly how much he could handle.

■

The problem was that by the time he started feeling a little drunk, it was too late. One night, David, Tom, Bert and Drake paid a guy $20 to buy them a 12-pack. Drake called it "talkin' beer"—not enough to get drunk on, but enough to loosen the tongue and make talking easier.

But the booze went too fast. So they returned to the convenience store where a cute college girl was at the cash register. Drake sweet-talked her while David bought two more 12-packs. She was too taken with Drake to embarrass herself—and him—by asking for an I.D. So she let it slide.

By 11 p.m., David couldn't remember how many drinks he'd had. More than six, but probably fewer than 10 ... at least he thought.

"Okay, that's enough, gentlemen," he announced with playful pomp. "It's been real. I gotta get home. See ya in the trenches of Tecumseh High."

He put the key in the ignition of his mom's Mustang without trouble. See? Not all that drunk, he muttered. He started the engine and slowly pulled into the street.

Whoa! Things were a little fuzzy and blurred. He opened his eyes wide, leaned forward and concentrated on the center line. It helped. Just keep the corner of the hood lined up on the center line, go slow, be cool and get home fit as a fiddle, he told himself.

With his eyes glued to the center line, he didn't notice the stop sign. And he didn't see the Mercury until after he'd broadsided it.

The next thing he remembered was sitting in the police station, holding a handkerchief to his bloody nose, and seeing his parents walk through the door to take him home.

Blind choice:
Without looking ahead, turn to page 74 or page 109 to see how his parents respond to his accident.

"Drake, wait up!" David ran across the street. Twice in the past two weeks, David had tried to talk to his friend. And both times Drake had cut him off with weak excuses. "Gotta run. Homework." Or "My mom's waitin' for me, Davey. Can't talk right now." This time David wouldn't be put off.

Drake watched David cross the street and shuffled from one foot to the other, his fingers stuffed into his jean pockets. His clothes were dirty, his hair unwashed and his nose running.

"Drake, we gotta talk ... Really."

"Yeah." Sniff. "Yeah, right." Sniff. "How ya doin', Davey?"

"How are *you* doin'?"

Sniff. "Hey! What you see is what you get."

"I don't like what I see, Drake. You look lousy. Are you sick? The flu?"

"Nah! Just tired. Puttin' in long hours, you know. Hittin' the books."

"Is that all you've been hittin', Drake?" David asked quietly.

"Aw, man! Can't you talk about anything else?"

"You came to me, remember? You said you needed help."

Sniff. "Yeah, right. And I do. But now's not a good time, Davey. After this semester, okay? We get through finals. Then I'll go straight. I'll get clean and sober for good." Sniff.

"Why wait, Drake?" David asked, feeling something like anger stirring in his stomach. "You aren't going to classes much. You failed the last tests."

"Look!" Drake said, starting to sound angry. "I said after the semester, okay? If you really want to help me you'll loan me a couple of bucks."

"What for?"

Drake rolled his eyes. He took a deep breath to calm himself and then spoke as if he were talking to a child. "Because, my friend, I'm hurtin'. I need something. Just one little white, and I'll be fine, see?"

David felt his heart sag. The booze and pills had taken over. And yet David's heart went out to his friend, standing there freezing in the cold. David wanted so much to give him the money. Or wrap him in his coat, take him home, feed him and tell him everything was okay.

But he couldn't. It wouldn't work. He knew that.

"No," he said finally. "No, Drake. I'm sorry."

Drake didn't beg or cry. Something like a shadow passed over his face. And whatever had been there was gone, replaced with undisguised hate. Drake leaned so close to David that David could smell his breath, rank with the smell of old booze. "Thanks for nothin' ... friend."

He turned and walked away.

David's heart nearly broke. Drake's alcoholism wasn't ruining just Drake's life. It was ruining his as well. It was like a silent, deadly virus that killed its host and crippled everyone else it touched.

What could he do now? David wondered. Maybe he should go back to his pastor, Jeff Marsh, for more advice. Or maybe it was too late. Maybe he couldn't do anything now.

What would you do?

If David gives up on Drake, turn to page 106.
If David returns to his pastor for advice, turn to page 38.

Even without the kids standing around it, the car would've stood out. A red Nissan sportscar. David didn't know the model, but it was a beauty—especially surrounded by the rust buckets in the student parking lot.

Not until the warning bell rang and the kids parted did David recognize the driver. "Hey, Drake," he said quietly, walking up to the driver's window.

The figure behind the steering wheel jerked his head up, fumbled madly with something in the passenger seat and started to get out.

"Hey, take it easy," David said, leaning against the door. "It's me."

"Oh, wow, Dave. Don't ever, ever sneak up on me like that." Drake leaned forward and reached under the car seat, sat up and looked out through all the windows before he relaxed a little. "So, what's up?"

David sighed and looked away. "What's up?" David responded. "You drop out of school, disappear for four months, then show up in a flashy car in the school parking lot. And you ask me what's up?"

What was wrong with Drake? He had bags under his eyes. His nose and lips were red. He had a short, punk haircut and an earring. "Drake, are you in some kind of trouble?" he finally asked.

"Me? Trouble? I got the man watchin' every move. I got my source makin' me deal at high schools, or he'll cut me off."

"You're dealing? Here ... at Tecumseh?"

"Tecumseh, Monroe, Brindelton. Every place ... Can you believe it?"

David couldn't. Drake acted as though dealing drugs at high schools was the most normal thing in the world. "Drake, what ..."

"I tell the guy, 'High schools are losers man. The cops got narcs undercover in high schools. Look just like the kids, only their grades aren't as good,' " Drake interrupted, all the while glancing in the mirror, looking out the windows, rubbing his hands against his thighs and sniffing.

David stepped back as though the car was contaminated. "Why, man?"

Drake rolled his bloodshot eyes. "Nickels and dimes. This baby didn't come from Santa, you know." He caressed the dashboard like a favorite pet.

David leaned down and looked closely. "Looks like most of your money's going up your nose, too, bro."

Drake wiped a tiny drop of blood from under his nose and shrugged. "Well, that too. You know—gettin' high and gettin' by." He started the engine. "Hey, gotta go, man. Can't stay in one place too long." With that he fishtailed out of the parking lot.

David felt a wave of depression sweep over him like a flood of hot syrup. They'd been best friends since fourth grade. Now it was all gone. The Drake he'd known was gone—dead. A small line of white powder was his only monument. An empty wine bottle was his only headstone.

Three weeks later, he learned Drake had been arrested selling crack. David stayed home in bed, depressed. He couldn't believe what had happened. He felt angry and guilty—like it was somehow his fault.

He struggled over what to do. He'd toss and turn at night, worried about himself and his friend. He could try to keep other kids at school from falling into the trap that caught Drake. But could he make a difference? Especially when he couldn't even sleep. Maybe a sleeping pill would help.

What would you do?

If David uses a drug to get over his own depression, turn to page 110.
If he decides to fight drug abuse, turn to page 77.

David sat at the breakfast table, his nose aching where it had hit the steering wheel, his leg screaming where he had skinned it somehow, and his body groaning all over from a hangover. His father sat across the table sipping coffee and reading the paper as though nothing had happened.

Only he wouldn't speak.

It had been nearly 10 hours since they'd picked David up, and he hadn't heard his father utter a single word. He was scared—really scared—of what his father would finally say when he chose to speak.

After another 15 minutes of silence, he couldn't stand it any longer and decided to break the silence himself. "Dad," he said. "I'm sorry ..."

"Can I have another cup of coffee, Joan?" his father asked.

David started to say something, but his father silenced him with a look. He folded his paper, sipped his coffee and leaned forward, staring into his cup. Finally, he looked up and spoke directly at David.

"Judgment error or personality flaw," he said. "I'm not sure which."

David wanted to say something but dared not.

"I hope it's the first," his father went on. "I hope you just made a mistake—drank too much. And then made a second mistake by driving."

"That's all ..."

John Pearce held up his hand. "But I'm not sure. If you'd just drunk too much and decided to stay where you were—or called me to come get you—I'd say, 'Well, David made a mistake. But at least he's mature enough to realize it.' Then we'd talk about it, you'd agree it was stupid, and it would be over."

David just looked at his father, afraid of what was coming next.

"But it didn't stop with the first mistake," Mr. Pearce said. "You compounded the first mistake of drinking, with a second: driving."

"I'm sorry, Dad. I ... I guess I never thought ..."

"Precisely, David!" his father interrupted. "You never thought."

David heard a crackling sound come from the stove and realized his mother was frying sausage. The smell wafted over him, and his stomach lurched. Why did she have to cook sausage when he was hung over? Why couldn't she just serve cold cereal and orange juice?

"You're not stupid, David," his father was saying. "Your grades prove that. You're smart—smarter than I was when I was your age."

David's head throbbed and his stomach rolled. If it wasn't empty, it would be soon. His dad set down his cup and shifted in his chair. David knew his sentence was coming now.

"So your mother and I have decided that—until we're convinced you've learned to think straight again—we're confiscating your car keys. That's the only way we can protect other people from your reckless, stupid choices."

His dad got up from the table and dumped his cold coffee in the sink. David just sat there. How would he respond to his parents' ultimatum?

What would you do?
If David decides not to drink again, turn to page 116.
If he rebels against the restrictions, turn to page 94.

JUST THIS ONCE

He made it home, somehow. Drove very slowly into the driveway, got out of the car, took two steps and passed out in the front yard.

His mother found him. "David?" Her voice was cold. "David, get up!"

He tried to stand. He was dizzy. He wanted to throw up. She didn't move to help him. "Come on, David ... Go take a shower, we'll talk about this when ... oh, my, you stink."

Finally, he made it to his feet, stumbled into the house and up to the shower. He let the hot water pound on him for a long time, took four aspirin, drank a glass of water and put on his robe.

When he got to the kitchen, his parents were eating breakfast. He poured a big glass of orange juice and sat down. His parents just kept eating. Saying nothing. Finally Dad finished his eggs and looked at David.

"You're nearly an adult—almost old enough to carry a gun in the Army."

"Dad, I ... "

"No, let me finish. What you did last night was foolish. And dangerous. You could've killed yourself—or someone else." He paused in thought.

"You know how we feel about drinking. But it's your life. If you get arrested or have a wreck, it's your problem. If you ... Well, I think you know what I mean. I hope you use the brain God gave you."

Dad stood and walked out. Mom followed. David felt empty. He knew he hadn't heard the last of this. And he knew he'd have to tell them something.

What would you do?

If David decides he can handle his drinking, turn to page 46.
If he decides to talk more about the issue, turn to page 60.

"You can't save the world, Davo. Why don't you lighten up?" Bert Roberts, the big tight end was putting away his books and collecting his coat from his locker. "Relax, dude."

David stood beside Bert and rocked from one foot to the other. "I'm not trying to save the whole world, Bert. Just some of my friends."

"What if they don't wanna be saved?" Bert asked, shutting his locker.

"Then they didn't see Drake. They didn't see what drugs did to him."

"Everyone's not Drake, Dave."

"No," David said, evenly. "Some are worse." He held out the clipboard to Bert. "So, you gonna sign or what?"

Bert looked down at the clipboard and made a face. "I dunno, man. I'm not much of a joiner. I'm kinda a loner, you know?"

"Look, I'm not asking you to join anything," David responded persistently. "All I'm asking you to do is sign this agreement that you won't drink or do drugs for this school year." He thrust the clipboard at his friend.

"I dunno."

"Well, what don't you know, Bert? You thinking of doing some crack this weekend? Is that it?"

Bert's face turned dark. "You know that's not it, and it's not funny to joke about it. Drake was my friend too. I'm never going near that stuff."

David shrugged. "So sign."

"I just don't want to come off as some kind of goody-goody. I don't want people to think ..."

"What will they think if they know you refused to sign?" David asked. He was immediately sorry he'd said it. This wasn't the way to end drug abuse. Threats and intimidation were for the other side. "I'm sorry, Bert. That wasn't fair. Think about it, okay? That's all I ask."

He turned and started away and felt Bert's big hand on his arm.

"Wait a minute," Bert said. "Gimme the paper. I'll sign it. What the heck. Guess I'm the first guy on the football team to sign one of these, huh?"

David smiled. "No, the whole defense has signed."

"You're kidding!"

"Nope. We'd like to be the first drug-and alcohol-free football team in the school's history." David was beaming. "Before long, I hope to put up a sign in the locker room: This is a Drug-Free Zone."

Bert shook his head. "So, what's next after the team? The cheerleaders?"

David looked down the hall at all the lockers and beyond, out the big double doors. "Next," he said. "The whole school."

They laughed together. Who could say?

The End

The reaction wasn't what David had expected. There were no taunts. No one trashed his locker. At first people teased him. But even that tapered off and then died completely.

People just kind of ... ignored him. Acted as if he wasn't even there. Kids he had thought were his friends turned their backs on him. They didn't get up and leave when he sat with them at lunch. But they didn't talk to him either.

The guys he sometimes rode to school with called less and less, until there were no calls anymore. The girls he flirted with in the library started paying attention to other guys.

At first, he told himself not to worry about it. He was too strong to let it bother him. But then, one day, Maggy Prestler—a partier who had a reputation for liking beer—asked him a question about a history assignment.

He fumbled around over the answer, dropped his pencil and lost his place in the book twice before he finally got it out. And he realized how badly he missed all his old friends.

About a week after the Maggy Prestler incident, Bobby Themes approached him in the locker room after P. E. "Uh, David?" Bobby said. He was a bright student who got along with everyone without being part of any one clique.

David looked up from his shoelaces. "Yeah?"

"Uh, I'm Bobby ... Bobby Themes." He smiled. "We've ... uh ... got this class together."

"Yeah, I know who you are, Bobby. You've got a good arm. Why didn't you go out for the baseball team? We could use a good center fielder this year."

Bobby smiled, a little embarrassed. "Nah ... I'm into fishing and ... I dunno."

"Yeah? Where d'you go?"

"Up to Clifton Lake, usually. We've got a boat ... Hey, listen, the bell's gonna ring, and I told 'em I'd ask you so ... well, the thing is ... "

David finished tying his shoe and stood. "Ask me what?"

"Well, some of us ... I mean ... there's a small group of us that were thinking ... Shees! This is hard." He ran his hand through his hair. "Some of us are thinking of starting a SADD—Students Against Driving Drunk—chapter here. And we were wondering if you'd, you know, help out."

Bobby looked at David apprehensively, as though he was

going to laugh or yell at him or something. David smiled and felt his heart warm at least 50 degrees. "I'd be glad to help, Bobby. Just tell me where to be and when."

"Really? Hey, great!" Bobby responded enthusiastically. "You're the first athlete we've gotten. This is great!"

And it was great. It felt good to have people who wanted him around. Maybe things are going to go right again, David thought to himself. Maybe he'd made the right choice, and things would turn out okay. He just wished he could do something to help Drake. He didn't even know where Drake was now.

Blind choice:
Without looking ahead, turn to page 18 or page 25 to continue the story.

"You sure you don't want a beer, Dave?" Warren Pence slurred for the 20th time. "You sure you don't wanna party down?"

"No, Warren, I'm fine," he answered for the 20th time.

The Pencer shook his head. "Diet Coke is *definitely* not a party drink, Davo. You've definitely gotta lighten up. Definitely." He walked away.

Was Warren drunk? Definitely this, definitely that. He must be drunk, David thought. Drunk and stupid! David wanted to slap him. Shock him. Make him see what he was doing. And while he was at it, he wanted to stand up on the porch railing and scream at all of them.

"What's the matter with all of you?" he'd yell at the top of his lungs. "The one night of your lives when you should act like adults—graduation night—you're acting like you haven't got a single brain cell among you." But he didn't yell anything. And he didn't slap Warren Pence. It probably wouldn't work anyway. Nothing else had.

For months, he and his friends had worked their tail ends off. Petitions, contracts, guest speakers, locker searches. Everything you could think of. And still, kids were taking drugs and drinking at parties like this one all over town on graduation night.

Finally, the group had gotten tired and given up. What was the use fighting it? Why invite ridicule trying to save people from something they didn't want to be saved from?

"Neat party, huh," John Metzger said, stepping up beside David. He was drinking a 7-Up.

"Yeah, some great blowout," David answered sarcastically. "On the successful party scale, I'd have to give this one an eight."

"Nope, a nine. That's how many people are passed out on the patio."

David shook his head. A car was just pulling out, and Rachael's car was finally unblocked. "Let's go," he said.

They decided to stop at the Blue Moon Diner for something to eat on the way home. Since high school kids didn't usually eat there, they knew it would be one place that wasn't full of drunk seniors.

It was a little out of the way, but the night was pleasant. Rachael put the top down on her mom's convertible, and they turned up a Top 40 station and sang along. They talked about the future, their parents and church.

All in all they were having a good time.

Until they turned onto Highway 63, four blocks up from the diner.

Lights. Red. Flashing. Two police cars. A fire truck. An ambulance.

But everyone was moving slowly. Not rushing around like you'd expect at an accident scene. Just standing around, talking, shaking their heads.

Rachael slowed down as they passed. David could hear them talking but couldn't understand. "Three bloody backs" or something. He turned and looked, in spite of himself. There was something familiar about the car wrapped around the telephone pole.

"Stop!" he yelled so suddenly that Sammy nearly fell out of the car.

But Rachael couldn't stop. The cop was waving her on by and saying, "Come on, come on. Keep moving."

"What was it?" Sammy asked as they passed the cop.

David felt his breath coming in gasps. A lump was forming in his chest. "The car. The blue one. It was Tom Fisher's."

"You sure?" John asked.

"I saw him leaving The Pencer's party with Bert Roberts and Brian Donnenworth a little before we did."

"I hope they're all right," Sammy said, looking over her shoulder. It was no use, they were too far away now.

David shook his head. Now he understood why none of the police or firemen or paramedics were moving quickly. He heard his breath catch in his throat as he tried to swallow a sob. And in his mind he heard the cop's voice again.

"Three body bags," he said, feeling the tears burning his eyes. "That's what the cop was telling the paramedic when we drove by."

"Oh, God!" said Sammy, taking David's hand.

They were dead. The realization hit him like a cold blast. It made his chest hurt and his head throb. Three of his buddies, guys he played football with and had talked to not an hour ago ... were dead. Three body bags. "It didn't make sense so I didn't think ..."

"It still doesn't make any sense," Sammy said. She was crying.

The End

JUST THIS ONCE

84 JUST THIS ONCE

The only way to do time is to kill time. That's what all the old cons said. That's how you survived in prison.

Watch television; read; work out; watch television. Don't think about getting out. Don't think about next week or even tomorrow. Just think about today. Keep out of trouble. Mind your own business.

It was the most depressing place David had ever seen or been in. And it was home for the next five years. Three if he kept out of trouble. Maybe 18 months if he was lucky. Maybe not. One day at a time.

His pastor, Jeff Marsh, started visiting him after he'd been in only a week or so. David sent word he didn't want any visitors. It was a lie. He was desperate, lonely and afraid. But he was ashamed too.

The second time, David went down to see Jeff. But David didn't say much.

Finally, the third time, he began talking to the persistent minister. About prison life, other cons, the guards. And the pastor kept coming back—twice, even three times, each month.

One day they spoke of David's parents. "They feel like they've failed you in some way." Jeff shrugged his shoulders and smoothed his mustache.

"Oh, Lord." David felt like crying. "Everything they ever taught me I threw right back in their faces. I humiliated them."

"They're pretty tough. They're doing all right."

"Yeah, sure," David said, not believing. "And where does your son go to college, Mr. Pearce? Oh, he doesn't go to college. He's in the state pen."

"Well," said Jeff, smiling. "They aren't exactly bragging about it. But they aren't hiding it either. They love you, you know."

"What's to love?" David turned in his seat.

"David, I don't quote scripture too much, but there's something in Romans 5:8 that you might need to hear again." Jeff cleared his throat. "But God has shown us how much he loves us—it was while we were still sinners that Christ died for us!"

David looked at him with a blank stare.

"Just think about it. Let me give it to you again." He did, reciting the words clearly. "I'm not going to preach or anything. I just want you to keep that verse with you until I get back. Think about what it means."

So David thought. He lay on his cot, staring at the ceiling of his room and let the words run through his mind.

Then, one night, when things had gotten quiet, he sat upright in bed. "Still sinners," he said aloud. "While we were still sinners..." He lay back down on his cot and felt the tears coming to the corners of his eyes. He got it! While we were still sinners, Christ died for us!

That was what Jeff was trying to tell him. Jeff, his parents, God—they all still loved him. Loved him even when he was causing them all that grief. And they'd continue to love him for the rest of his life.

Even as the tears flowed down his cheeks, David began laughing. It started as a chuckle and built into a rolling, rumbling laugh. It felt good. He hadn't laughed in a long time.

Life would be a lot different now, he thought. A whole lot different.

The End

David stood in the phone booth drumming his fingers on the glass. "Come on, Drake, be there," he muttered into the phone.

"Hello!"

"Drake? David here."

"Yo, Davo-o-o-o-o! What can I do for you, my man?"

"I need someplace to go," David said, switching the phone to his other ear. "My parents threw me out."

"Whoa! Heavy duty! Say ... Have a drink and forget about it. They'll change their minds." He sounded impatient.

David shifted the phone again. "Easy for you to say. Can you help me, you know ... give me something to tide me over?"

"I gave you speed last night."

"Yeah, I know. But I don't need speed. I need to calm down. Something like ... you know ... Ludes ... Quaaludes."

"Sure. What are friends for? But ... uh ... they'll cost. They don't come cheap." They haggled over price for a while, and David was about to give up. He couldn't afford Drake's price. Then, suddenly, Drake had an idea.

"Hey, I got it. Sell those whites I gave you. Then I can share some of my ludes with you."

"Sell 'em?" David didn't know anything about selling.

"Sure! Easy as falling off a log. You know Roller World?"

"Yeah."

"Well, those teeny boppers are always looking to score. I do some of my best cash-and-carry business over there. Just flash a couple of pills near the snack bar, and you're in business."

So 30 minutes later, David was sitting in the snack bar of Roller World, listening to disco music, drinking a diet Coke and trying to figure out how to sell his pills. A couple of parents were standing at the rail at the other end, watching the little kids skate.

It wasn't as hard as he thought. Within 10 minutes a couple of junior high kids—hard cases with leather jackets and dirty blue jeans—walked in. They clearly weren't here to roller skate. One of them was smoking a cigarette.

They slid into a booth, ordered Cokes and just sat there, looking cool. Finally, David got up and walked over.

"You guys ... " his voice caught, and he cleared his throat. "You guys looking to score?"

"Cigarette" looked up at him through hooded eyes, his head cocked to one side. "Whataya sellin'?"

JUST THIS ONCE 87

David could feel his heart beating in his chest, and his hand shook as he reached into his own jacket pocket to get the pill bottle. He wished he had a drink or something.

He held the pills out and shook them intentionally so they couldn't see the tremor in his hand. "Speed," he said.

Cigarette regarded the brown bottle. "They any good?"

David snorted a laugh. "Get you going and keep you going."

"Let's see 'em."

He opened the childproof lid and tilted the bottle to each kid. "They're yours for $25," he said.

"We got $20."

David nodded his head. That would do just fine. The kid reached into his jacket pocket and pulled out a handful of wadded bills and began to count them on the table.

When the $20 was counted out David reached for it. Finally! Maybe now he could score some ludes. He reached to put the money in his pocket, and a huge hand grabbed his wrist.

"Just put your hands on the table and spread your legs," a voice said.

David tried to look around, but another hand pushed his head forward. Then his hands were jerked behind him and he felt cold metal go around each wrist. He was jerked back to his feet and spun around.

A big guy in a sweatshirt—a guy he had thought was a parent of one of the little kids—was standing in front of him reading from a little card. "You are under arrest," he recited. "You are accused of possession of a controlled substance, possession with intent to sell, selling a controlled substance, contributing to the delinquency of a minor ... "

He looked up at David, shook his head and looked down again. Now he was reading verbatim from the card. "You have the right to remain silent. Anything you say can and will be used against you in a court of law. You have the right to an attorney. If you cannot afford one ... "

David began to cry. What would happen now?

Blind choice:

Without looking ahead, turn to page 84 or page 89 to continue the story.

88 JUST THIS ONCE

"I never knew ..." was all Drake could say.

Mrs. Underwood started to get up and go to him, but Mr. Underwood stopped her with a hand on her arm. He took off his glasses and polished them with his tie as he said, "We packed a suitcase for you, son. It's in the car. Coach Clark said he would explain things for you at school."

Slowly, Drake stood and walked to his father. "Thanks Dad. Let's go."

Mr. Underwood looked up at him, raised his eyebrows in a question. Drake smiled back at him. "Let's go to Dr. Frieze's clinic," he said.

A collective sigh ran through the entire room. Dr. Frieze got up and walked over to Drake. "I'll drive you, Drake," he said. "This is your battle, and you have to fight it by yourself. Your parents will come see you in a couple of days. And later they'll join us in some programs. But for now, it's just you and me."

Drake shrugged his shoulders and turned to leave. As he and Dr. Frieze walked through the door, Drake turned and looked back into the room. "Thanks, everybody," he said.

Blind choice:
Without looking ahead, turn to page 96 or page 107 to learn what happens to Drake.

"Oh, David. You look so pale," his mother said. She reached across the table and took his hand.

The guard materialized at her side. "No physical contact with the inmates, ma'am," he said. Then the guard saw the tears forming in her eyes. "I ... uh ... I'm sorry. Regulations." He turned and walked away, watching the other prisoners in the visiting area of the county jail youth wing.

David hated this. The jail, the other prisoners, the guard. And these visits with his parents. His mother crying, his father trying to look calm.

"Are they treating you okay?" his father asked.

David nodded. "Fine."

"We brought you some candy," his mother said, and started to give him a box of candy bars. David waved to the guard, who looked over, saw the candy and nodded.

"Thanks," was all David could say. He looked at the clock. He wanted so much to hug his mom. But he didn't dare. If the other guys saw it and thought he was weak ... well, you didn't want to appear weak in here.

Mr. Pearce caught his glance at the clock and stood. "Well, we don't want to hog the visiting hour. Jeff Marsh is waiting. Come on, honey." He took his wife's arm. "Hang in there, son. Ninety days isn't such a long time."

Jeff Marsh's visit wasn't too bad. He didn't preach or pray or do anything that might make David look bad. He just talked.

He talked about God, but that was okay. He talked about God not holding grudges and being like that father in the story of the prodigal son—always waiting and watching for his children to return.

He said God had already forgiven David. All David had to do was admit he'd been wrong, forgive himself and accept God's forgiveness.

And that was the end of that. David had been in jail less than a month, but he'd learned fast. No one here ever admitted being wrong. That was a sure sign of weakness. And there was no way David Pearce was going to be weak. Not here. Not when he got out, either. No sir. If jail was teaching him anything, it was teaching David Pearce that being weak didn't pay.

Right now, David just wanted to get rid of Jeff and get back to the rec room. That's where Reggie hung out. And Reggie was the man to see if you needed something to help you mellow out.

The candy bars his mother had brought him would be just the ticket. Probably buy enough pills to get him through another week—until his parents came for another visit. Next time he'd ask for some money.

"... all a matter of being strong enough to be weak. Weak in the eyes of God," Jeff Marsh was saying.

"Yeah, Jeff. Hey, thanks," David said. He stood and walked away without looking back. He hated these visits!

Blind choice:
Without looking ahead, turn to page 102 or page 129 to see what happens when David gets out of prison.

"I understand how students feel," Mr. Hamner said after David expressed his concern about the locker searches. Mr. Hamner leaned forward and rested his arms on his big, oak desk. "But this is a war we're fighting. Some sacrifices have to be made."

David swallowed and tried to wet his lips. He'd never expressed an opinion to a vice principal before. "I know, Mr. Hamner. It's just that we're treating people like criminals or something. You searched the lockers of kids who've never touched alcohol—much less drugs."

"We have to be impartial. We can't just search a few lockers."

"But what about rights?" David said, getting a little courage now. "Just because we're minors, does that mean we don't have any rights?"

"What rights are we talking about, David?"

"Well, like the right to privacy. And unlawful search and seizure."

"There's nothing unlawful about searching lockers. The courts ... "

"But, Mr. Hamner, don't you have to have evidence that someone's doing drugs before you can break into that person's locker?"

"You've raised a couple of different issues there." The vice principal leaned back in his chair. "Let's take them one at a time. First, we didn't break into the lockers. We used a master key. Second, they aren't your lockers. They belong to the school district. We just let the students use them."

"Well, shouldn't that be explained?" David interrupted. "I mean—that they aren't ours and you can look in them whenever you please? Some people keep personal stuff in their lockers ... "

"Tell me about it," said Mr. Hamner, smiling.

"Not illegal stuff or anything. But personal. Stuff they don't want other people seeing. Maybe if they knew the lockers weren't private, they could take out the personal stuff."

Mr. Hamner rubbed his bald head in thought. "Okay," he said at last. "I'll agree to that. We let students know that we can search lockers at our discretion. But, David, we're not going to tell people when we're inspecting. Surprise inspections are the only way to keep drugs and alcohol out. Okay?"

"I guess."

"Is there something else?"

"No...Well, yeah. It's just... I still feel like a suspect. You're saying until the problem's gone, we'll all be treated like potential pushers."

Mr. Hamner sighed. "I know what you mean. I don't like it either. This is no way to run a school—treating your students like criminals." He turned his chair slightly and looked out the window.

"Oh, how I wish we could just teach again! No one ever told us we'd have to be probation officers, cops and narcs. Teaching's just one of the things we have to do." He turned back and looked at David. "But, my friend, that's the way it is. And until this drug thing is gone from Tecumseh High School, we all have to give up something we want."

David just looked at Mr. Hamner. He didn't know what to say.

"I'm open to alternatives," Hamner offered. "You get any better ideas, you let me know. I understand you have some kids interested in doing something. Maybe they'll have ideas. Maybe we can join forces."

"You mean students and teachers?"

"Yeah, and parents too. A united front of kids, teachers and parents. Community leaders, too, maybe."

"My pastor would help."

"There you go! Take it to your friends. See if they can come up with a better plan. I'll listen."

■

"So, what do you think?" David asked the group of six kids who'd responded to his fliers announcing a meeting of students concerned about alcohol and drugs in school.

"Join forces with the teachers? Are you crazy?" asked John Metzger. "We'd be laughed out of the school. Kids'll call us narcs!"

"Maybe not," Rachael Thomas said. "Not if we make it the 'in' thing."

Sammy Wu shook her head. "Staying sober will never be 'in.' Not as long as half the kids are drinking and the other half would if they could."

"I dunno," John said. "I mean, joining the teachers..."

"It's such a big problem," Sammy said. "Maybe we ought to just be a support group for each other and not worry about changing the world."

"So, we give up?" Rachael asked the group. "We just worry

about ourselves and to heck with everyone else?"

"How much do you think they worry about us?" Sammy asked.

No one answered. They all looked at David. What would he suggest?

What would you do?
If he says they can't do anything, turn to page 119.
If he urges them to keep trying, turn to page 140.

"So, you can't sleep?" Drake asked.

"Yeah. My folks took my car keys and told me to straighten out," David said. He shifted the phone to his other ear.

"Sounds like my old man. He used to try that stuff on me."

"Well, I can't handle them treating me like a little kid or something," David said, frustrated.

"Why don't you come on over, and we'll mellow out?" Drake offered.

David sighed. "I said, man: no wheels. They took my keys."

"Not to worry. Dr. Drake to the rescue. Be there in 10, Davo."

David told his dad he was going for a walk—to think. Drake picked him up two houses down, and they drove to Drake's "fort"—an abandoned hunting cabin. Drake brought a six-pack and a bottle of Jim Beam bourbon he filched from his dad's liquor cabinet. "He'll never miss it. He doesn't drink Beam anyway. Someone gave it to him for Christmas."

They drank it all.

■

"So, you don't remember any of it?" Jeff Marsh asked. They were sitting in the pastor's living room.

"No. I don't remember passing out. I don't remember how I got home and past my parents without them seeing me ..."

"Maybe you didn't. Maybe they did see you," Jeff said.

"No. They were too surprised when they came into my room."

"They didn't expect you to be there?"

"I don't think so. And not in the shape I was in."

"How's that?"

"I don't remember throwing up, Jeff. But I sure did. All over myself, my bed, my pillow. That's the scariest thing. I read about this guy who threw up in his sleep and strangled on ..."

"I get the picture," Jeff interrupted. "So they walked in and saw you."

"No, I'd come to and found myself in the mess. I was stripping the bed and trying to clean up. I don't know what I thought I'd do with the stuff."

Jeff leaned back and crossed his legs. "And they threw you out."

"Yeah. Usually my dad just gets real quiet when he's mad.

But this time he hit the ceiling. Screaming, yelling. I've never seen him like that."

"I didn't know where to go. So I came here," David said.

"Yeah," Jeff said. "I'm glad you did. So, what now?"

David shrugged his shoulders, played with his empty Coke can. "That's what I'm asking you."

"Why don't you call 'em, David? Whataya got to lose?"

"Maybe my life," he quipped, trying to be lighthearted. But inside he was torn apart. Should he—could he—go to his parents now?

What would you do?
If David agrees to talk to his parents, turn to page 60.
If David refuses to call his parents, turn to page 86.

"My name is Drake..."

"Hi, Drake," everyone said together.

"... and I'm an alcoholic." The word almost stuck in his throat. Not bad, just a little click. It was getting easier every time.

At first he'd tried to deny it. He wasn't an alcoholic. That's what those old guys down on Wooster Place were—the ones who slept in doorways and tried to clean your windshield for a quarter when you stopped at the traffic light. They were alcoholics. Drake had seen himself as just a kid who occasionally drank too much.

That's what he'd tried to tell himself, over and over again. "... until I believed it. Almost believed it," he said to the group sitting in front of him. "But I knew it was a lie even then."

His mom and dad were in the audience. And David and a couple of others from church. They were smiling now, and he smiled too. "Well, I'm not lying anymore. I'm telling the truth. I'm telling it to you and to my family and friends, here tonight. And I'm telling it to myself."

He took a breath and started to say it loudly, then changed his mind, let out some of the breath and spoke in almost a whisper. "I ... am ... an ... alcoholic. If I start drinking again, I wouldn't quit. It would kill me. I have a disease called alcoholism. And if I lie about it, I'll die."

It wasn't much of a speech, David thought to himself. But, then it didn't have to be. It was the truth. "And the truth will set you free," he murmured, remembering his favorite passage from the book of John.

■

That was Drake's first sober speech. But it was far from his last. He spoke wherever he could get an audience. At church. At home. At student council meetings.

And always the message was the same: The easiest way to beat substance abuse is not to start. Not "Just Say No!" he'd say. That made it sound easy, and it wasn't easy. Sometimes it seemed impossible. But you did it anyway ... because it was smart.

You should treat drugs like a killer you might meet on the street: You leave them alone. You walk way out around them, and you never look back.

That's how you beat drugs and alcohol.

The End

"Drake!?" The guy huddled in the alley looked up at David for a second, pulled himself up and ran into the building, slamming the door behind him. "Drake, wait!"

April began warm—in the 80s—and Sammy Wu, John Metzger and David had decided to pick up cones at Monroe Dairy Delicacies.

John looked at Sammy and shrugged. "Wha'cha got?" John asked.

"Raspberry ripple. You?" She licked her ice cream cone.

"Butter pecan," John said. "Wanna lick?" He held it out to her.

"Nah. Better not mix 'em." They laughed as they walked toward the alley. David was about halfway down it, trying to open an old door. "David? What're you doing? Where's your cone?"

David looked up at them. "It was Drake. I saw him!"

John shook his head. "Drake joined the Marines, David. Remember?"

David walked back to his friends. "No he didn't. His father checked."

"I heard he joined the Hell's Angels," Sammy said.

"That stuff's just rumors," David snapped back. "I'm telling you I just saw him. It didn't look like him at first ... "

"Who'd it look like?" John asked.

"Well, like a street person—older than Drake and kinda sick. Dirty."

"Then how'd you know it was him?" Sammy asked.

"He had on Drake's letter jacket."

"Maybe Drake sold it. Or gave it to the Salvation Army."

"No, it still had the pins on it—awards and stuff."

They were silent for a moment, thinking. John said, "David, this is crazy. What would Drake be doing in an alley in downtown Monroe?"

"He was crying," David said. "It was like ... I dunno ... like this long, high-pitched, whining sound. And it went on and on. That's why I looked ... " He let it drop there. A lump in his throat made it hard to talk.

Sammy lowered her cone from her mouth and stepped up to David. She looked closely at his face and asked, "David, what else was he doing?"

David shook his head and began to cry. He leaned against the wall.

"David, please. We're his friends too."

He covered his face with his hands and then ran them through his hair.

"David?"

"He was sticking a needle in his arm!" David blurted out. "Aw, Sammy. He was shooting up. And ... and he ran inside when he saw me."

They drove home in near silence. No radio. Little conversation. Occasionally, one of them would remember some silly thing Drake had done and mention it. They'd smile. Then David or Sammy would be crying again. What had begun as a nice, clean, warm, spring day had now become a descent—however brief—into the private hell of drug addiction.

David called in sick on Monday. When Sammy called to check on him, he said he was too upset to see people. He didn't know what to do.

David knew he had to do something. Maybe a sleeping pill would help him rest. He hadn't slept since Saturday. Or maybe he should use his emotional energy to urge other people at school to avoid drugs.

What would you do?
If David uses a drug to deal with his grief, turn to page 110.
If he decides to fight drug abuse, turn to page 77.

"Naw, Pence, I really can't," David said, embarrassed.

"Sorry you'll miss the fun," Pence said. "If you get thirsty, let me know." And he walked away.

David and Rita walked around, hand in hand. People congratulated him. But somehow the words didn't mean as much when people smelled like alcohol. As he watched his friends drink, David wasn't sure why everyone said it was so fun. Things were getting out of control.

Someone spilled beer on the white sofa in the living room.

A loud crash came from the basement family room, followed by a girl's high-pitched scream and a chorus of giggles.

Someone got sick in the flower bed by the front porch.

It got to be too much for David. The amount of drinking and the effect it was having troubled him. He started to say something, but stopped himself. He didn't want to ruin this night with a bunch of worries.

So he was thankful when Rita suggested they leave.

As they walked toward the car, Rita said, "I've never been able to understand why kids drink so much."

"I know what you mean," David muttered, relieved she felt like he did. "I mean, it seems so stupid. So dangerous."

"Not to mention illegal," Rita added.

As they drove and talked, they decided they needed to talk to someone about the problem. David suggested they talk to his pastor, Jeff Marsh. Maybe he'd have ideas.

David kissed Rita goodnight, and went home with his excitement about Rita clouded by the alcohol abuse he'd seen that night.

■

Jeff had his feet up on his desk and was reading the comics when David stuck his head into the office that Sunday after church.

"Jeff? Uh, you got a minute?"

The minister lowered the paper and looked over the top of his glasses. David felt like laughing. Jeff looked 20 years older than his 30-something years when he looked over the top of his glasses like that.

"Sure, David. Come on in. I was just unwinding a little."

He folded the paper neatly and threw it in a corner. "Have to save the comics. My kids hate it when I mess 'em up."

David entered the office, holding Rita's hand. He introduced

Rita, who Jeff had seen at several football games.

David and Rita sat in the two rocking chairs across from Jeff's messy desk. Instead of asking what they wanted to talk about, Jeff just lowered his chin and looked over the top of his glasses again. This time he raised his eyebrows and looked like he was another 10 years older.

"We were at this party the other night," David began.

"Pencer—Warren Pence, this nerdy guy at school," Rita interrupted. "He threw this party. With beer and everything."

David didn't seem to notice the interruption. "His parents provide beer for his parties so he can make friends," she said.

Jeff leaned back in his chair. "Does it work?" he asked.

"Well," David said. "A lot of people show up. But they only come for the beer. They don't care anything about Pencer."

This time Rita interrupted. "You should see what they did to his house. They trashed the place. It was awful."

Jeff Marsh laced his fingers behind his head. "And your concern is?" He just let it hang there.

"How can people do that? They get drunk every weekend," David said.

"And then they drive," Rita added.

David leaned forward in his chair. "They get into fights. They get sick. Drake Underwood was so hung over, he could hardly keep his eyes open in Sunday school this morning."

"Drugs?" Jeff asked.

"Everywhere!" Rita said earnestly. "Last week, at the dance, you needed a gas mask just to walk through the restrooms. And it was like a pharmacy in there. I've never seen so many pills!"

"Even in the locker rooms," David said, shaking his head. "You'd think athletes would be wise to that stuff."

David was obviously frustrated and shaken by his own reports. "What can we do, Jeff? Any ideas?"

Jeff took off his glasses and tossed them on a huge stack of papers. He massaged the bridge of his nose, smoothed his thick, black mustache. "How about SADD—Students Against Driving Drunk? That would be a start."

David shook his head. "I've heard of it. But I wouldn't know how to start it at Tecumseh. Besides, people don't think it's a big problem. You know, something really bad has to happen before they'll do anything."

Jeff picked up a pencil and rummaged around until he found a small notebook on the desk. "Well, if you guys are concerned, I'd bet some others are just as worried as you are. Why don't you bring it up at the youth group this week. Or maybe student council?"

"I guess we could mention it at student council—that would be the logical place, I think," David said. "You know, test the waters."

"Yeah," Rita nodded. "We have a meeting on Tuesday. Maybe I could bring it up ... just to see if there's any interest."

"Okay," Jeff said, still writing. "I know a guy in Monroe who started a SADD chapter. I'll call and see if he has any suggestions. Fair enough?"

They agreed. They'd throw out the alcohol and drug problem as a concern at student council meeting and see if there was enough interest to do anything about it.

■

There was and there wasn't interest. Some kids agreed with David and Rita. Some didn't. What's the big deal, they asked? Every school in the country had drugs and alcohol around. It was something you had to live with.

All council members, however, agreed to consider that there might be a problem. They were going to appoint a fact-finding committee, but then the bell rang, ending the meeting.

So they all agreed to think about it and decide later what to do.

David and Rita left the meeting partly encouraged and partly discouraged. At least people had listened. But they hadn't done anything. And now another week would go by—enough time for everyone in school to learn what had been said ... and who had said it.

Blind choice:
Without looking ahead, turn to page 25 or page 118 to see how students react to David and Rita's concern.

JUST THIS ONCE

They called him Skin because he'd shaved his head once. That was about five years ago, but the name stuck. He didn't mind. Down here everyone had a street name, and "Skin" was better than most.

Better than Rudy 354 or Swami or Jungle Muffin. He had no idea how those people got their names. They probably didn't either. And they didn't care. They were all crackheads. They didn't care about anything much, except getting another vial of crack cocaine. Smoke it. Mellow out. Get another.

Skin wore a navy pea-coat and a black stocking-cap. He thought it made him look "bad"... which it did. And looking bad was important to Skin for two reasons. First, because he was a coward. Second, he sold crack cocaine for a living. Rudy 354, Swami and Jungle Muffin were his steadiest customers. And they *were* bad. They'd kill you for a vial of crack.

Skin never touched crack. He did a line of coke sometimes... to relax when he went home. And he drank beer and whiskey boilermakers like a fish. But not crack. That stuff was poison.

But business was business. So, here he was, standing outside the Li'l Heaven Bar on Wooster Place pushing crack cocaine.

But, Lord, it was cold and he wanted to go home. If only Dave the Dude would show up. My, but that boy did buy some crack! Oh, Rudy 354 and Swami and Jungle Muffin were steady customers. But that Dave the Dude. He was a... a... Skin searched his mind for the right word. Windfall! That's what he was. He'd come down about twice a week and buy maybe $1,000 worth of crack. Sometimes three times a week. He must be sellin' it, Skin thought.

Well, that was fine, s'long as he wasn't sellin' it on Skin's corner. Man couldn't be expected to smoke it all hisself.

But he was smokin' some of it. Just look at him, comin' down the street right now. Weavin' back and forth and lookin' bad. Wearin' that school jacket with all them awards on it like he was some kinda jock. He musta picked up that jacket in a trash bin somewheres. All dirty and torn and smelly like that. Lord! And way too big for him with them skinny shoulders.

Dave the Dude walked right up to Skin and held out a big wad of money without saying a word. Man's got guts, Skin thought. Might as well just put a big sign on my back: "Crack Sold Here."

Skin counted the money and handed a plastic bag of crack vials to Dave the Dude who looked at it, looked over his shoulder, looked back at it and licked his lips. Then he turned and started walking, as quickly as his shaking legs could carry him, toward the abandoned warehouse.

Look at that, Skin said to himself. Boy's got a name on the back of that coat. He tried to read the name, but the dirt and grease made it hard.

Then, finally he got it. Pearce. Coat says Pearce. Wonder who that Pearce was an' why he threw away his coat? Hey, maybe Dave the Dude is Pearce. Maybe that's his righteous handle.

Skin laughed at the idea. Nah! Whoever Pearce was it couldn't have been Dave the Dude. That Pearce guy was somebody—an athlete who played football and stuff. Look at a boy like Dave the Dude, an' you knew he ain't never seen a football, much less play with one.

The End

"We *do* care about you!" David argued.

"No you don't!" Drake shouted back. "All you care about is you. Your reputation. You don't want to be seen with me."

"That's not true, and you know it. I do care about you. And so do your friends and your parents."

"Bull!"

"It's not bull, Drake. And if all that isn't enough, God cares about you. You have to believe that. We've grown up in this church together."

Drake shook his head and sat down behind the steering wheel. Finally, he looked up at David. "You're so naïve."

"Because I believe God loves us? and cares about us? and wants what's best for us? Does that make me naïve, Drake?"

Drake paused. "Yeah," he said, smiling disdainfully.

"Why, Drake? Why is it so hard to believe people really love you? That God cares about you?" David was surprised by his passion. He'd never talked this openly about his faith before.

Drake didn't answer. He just shook his head.

"Why can't you accept that people care about you?" David prodded.

Finally, Drake looked up at David. He leaned his head back against the headrest, closed his eyes and massaged his temples with his fists. "You really don't understand, do you? You don't get it."

That wasn't what David had expected. "Understand what?"

When his eyes opened, they were blazing again. The anger was back. "If he loves me so much, why'd he let it get like this?"

Whoa! David hadn't expected this. If who loves me? Let what get like this? He was off balance. "I, uh ... "

But Drake went on before David could say anything else. "You think I *like* waking up sick, puking all over myself? You think I *like* spending all day in school waiting for last bell so I can get to the bottle I've got stashed by the dumpster?"

"I didn't know ... "

"That's right, buddy. You don't know. You don't know anything!"

Drake's intensity was building. "You don't know what it's like waking up in your front yard and not knowing how you got there. You don't know what it's like hanging out with guys you can't stand—because they can buy beer."

"I'm sorry..."

"You don't know anything about me." He put on a pouting face and whined, "But Drake, God lo-o-o-o-oves you."

"He does, Drake. I know..."

"Then why can't I quit?" Drake shouted. Several people walking across the parking lot stopped and looked their way. David ignored them and started to say something, but Drake was still talking.

"It's all I think about. It's all I want to do. And I hate it." Two tears dripped down his cheeks. "Oh, God, I hate it! Why can't God help me quit? "I've asked him. I've prayed every prayer I know. But nothing changes." Now his face was wet with tears. "I can't keep living like this."

David didn't know what to say. "Maybe if you talked to someone," he stammered.

Drake looked up, seriously. The tears were gone now. All that was left was a sad longing. "That's what I'm doing, David. I'm talkin' to you." He held up his hand as if to salute.

David hesitated a moment, then reached out, locked thumbs with Drake and clasped the hand in his own. "We're in this together, bud," he said resolutely.

He'd help Drake beat this thing, he told himself as he walked away. Somehow. Maybe the two of them could work together. They wouldn't have to get anyone else involved. Or maybe he should get outside help. After all, he hadn't known what to say when Drake told him. How could he help alone?

What would *you* do?
If David asks someone to help, turn to page 132.
If David tries to help Drake by himself, turn to page 63.

106   JUST THIS ONCE

David's arms burned. He could feel the muscles beginning to knot, and perspiration stung his eyes. Finally, he couldn't lift the weights off his chest.

"Done," he gasped. "Take it."

Don Burrows, his workout partner, took the weights and placed them on the rack above the bench. He looked down at David's face and tossed him a towel. "You goin' for the Mr. Universe title?"

"Just decided to work hard today. Sweat the poison out of my system, I guess."

"Tell me about it. You're makin' us all look bad. Take it easy! You're gonna kill someone."

David wiped the sweat from his face and breathed deeply. Yeah, he was gonna kill someone, okay. He was gonna kill Mr. Drake Get-Off-My-Back Underwood. Only he couldn't kill Drake. So he was working out his anger and frustration on the weights instead.

Okay, Drake, he thought as he walked to the chinning bar. I'm off your back. I got problems of my own, and I don't need yours too. So you handle them yourself. They're your problems.

He chuckled to himself at a perverse thought. Kill him? I don't have to kill him, David realized. He's doing a fine job by himself.

Blind choice:
Without looking ahead, turn to page 72 or page 97 to continue the story.

Six weeks after Drake entered Eastside Clinic, his parents brought him home. David was there to meet him. They shook hands formally in front of Drake's parents, and then headed for Drake's apartment above the garage where they could talk.

"You look great," David said, sitting at the desk.

"Bull," said Drake, flopping on the bed. "I gained 15 pounds." Drake jumped up off the bed and paced around the room, looking out the windows, patting his hands on his thighs.

"Something wrong?" David asked.

"Nah ... I dunno ... I'm just stir crazy. Been locked up too long." He paced back and forth in the room. "Hey, let's go for a drive."

David shrugged. "Sure. Where d'you wanna go?"

Drake was already halfway down the stairs. "I'll think of someplace."

David followed, a little hesitantly. Something was wrong. When he'd visited him at the clinic he'd seemed different. But now ... No, it was probably just excitement at being out of the clinic and back in the real world. After all, Drake was still Drake.

They cruised around town, talking. Football, girls, music, school, teachers. Suddenly Drake shouted, "Pull over! Stop the car!"

David pulled to the curb. He didn't see anything or anyone he knew. They were about two blocks off Wooster Place, famous for its drugs and prostitution. It wasn't a part of town where David spent much time. He wasn't sure how he'd gotten here. But Drake must've seen somebody he knew.

While David was thinking, Drake jumped out of the car and jogged up to a guy in front of a seedy-looking bar called the Li'l Heaven Bar. The guy was seedy-looking too. Tall, with a stocking cap up on the top of his head. He was rail-thin and had a three-day growth of beard.

How did Drake know this guy? They were talking intensely. Drake gestured as he talked, but the guy hardly moved. Then one of the guy's hands came out of his pocket, and he shook Drake's hand. Only it didn't look like he was shaking hands, really. More like he was doing something that was supposed to look like shaking hands.

That was it. They dropped hands, and Drake's went immediately to his own pocket. The guy had given him something. Drake's left hand shot out and stuffed something down the front

108 JUST THIS ONCE

of the guy's shirt ... Money!

David's mind went totally blank. Not because he didn't know what Drake had just bought from the guy, but because he didn't want to know. How could this be? Had Drake just been conning everyone? lying? biding his time until he could get back down here and buy more pills?

Drake was coming toward the car, the hint of a smile—almost a smirk—on his face. It was true. He'd tricked David into driving him down here to buy drugs.

Drake was still 10 feet from the car when David quickly put it in gear and sped away. David didn't know what else to do. And he didn't know what would happen to Drake now.

Blind choice:
Without looking ahead, turn to page 72 or page 18 to learn what happens to Drake.

JUST THIS ONCE   109

David's parents didn't take him home. They had a suitcase in the car, and they took him to the Beacon, a shelter next to the YMCA. They drove in silent, seething anger.

When the car pulled up to the door, David's dad got out, opened the trunk and put the suitcase on the curb. Then he opened David's door and said: "Don't come home until you're clean and sober and can stay that way."

David was in shock. He couldn't believe his parents could do that to their only son. He stayed in the shelter all night—even though it made him more sick to his stomach than he already was.

The next morning, he sat in Jeff Marsh's living room and recounted his experience to his pastor.

"Shees, Jeff," he said. "It's awful. Full of old winos and junkies. I thought I was gonna lose it."

"Then today..."

"I hitched over here as soon as I could," David finished the sentence. "I gotta get outa there, Jeff. Can you help me?" David rubbed the bridge of his broken nose and winced at the pain.

The pastor looked at him over the top of his glasses. "No."

David felt his mouth fall open. "No!?"

Jeff shook his head. "No, David. You have to help yourself."

"How! That's what my parents keep saying! 'Help yourself. Help yourself.' But... but what am I supposed to do?"

"Maybe your parents are right, though. You're responsible for your own choices," Jeff suggested.

"Sure!" David replied sarcastically. "I guess that's why my parents always run my life."

"What would happen if you showed them you were responsible enough on your own?" Jeff asked patiently.

"I dunno."

"Think about it." Jeff's gaze drifted to the game playing silently on the television. "I can't make the decision for you."

David got up to leave. He was tired of adults constantly telling him to "be responsible... Make up your own mind." Were drugs and alcohol as bad as everyone made them out to be? Besides, couldn't he stop if he wanted to?

What would you do?

If David decides to stop using alcohol and drugs, turn to page 116.
If David keeps using alcohol and drugs, turn to page 129.

"Here come da crim'nal," he said, laughing in that high-pitched, wheezing laugh through his nose.

"Ain't he a frightening sight, though!" the other one remarked. He didn't laugh. Just smiled and shook his wooly head. He took a long pull on his ever-present cigarette and coughed.

One was Smith; the other Jones. Those weren't their real names, but that's what everyone at the Sanitation Department called them. Smith was about 50, tall and painfully thin. Jones was about 50 and thin—at least when you looked at him from the back. From the side he looked pregnant. Smith had a gold tooth right in front. Jones had no visible teeth at all.

They'd worked together on the same collection truck, picking up trash for 24 years. They liked their work and, in spite of their appearance, they worked hard, were reliable and were honest.

They were also the team to which the city assigned minors who had to do community service because they'd gotten in trouble with the law. Smith and Jones loved the assignments. They knew that these kids thought they were too good for this kind of work and looked down on them. So Smith and Jones took every opportunity to razz the smart-aleck high schoolers.

Today, the smart-aleck high school kid was David Pearce. "Hey, dope fiend," Smith said, winking at Jones. "Think we mighta come across some weed in a dumpster a couple a blocks back. Wanna climb in and look for it?"

"Yessir!" Jones said. "Maybe we can just forget this ol' garbage an' get high." He wheezed again in laughter.

David didn't reply. He threw his bag into the cab, pulled on his coveralls and tugged on his gloves. He hated this!

"Well, Jones," Smith said. "Looks like the crim'nal's ready to work."

Jones hopped into the cab and inched the truck up the alley. David began picking up the cans and emptying them into the collection bin on the tailgate. He tried not to think of the work. He thought it was degrading, stupid and filthy. Easier to just let his mind wander.

It was all Drake's fault. And his parents'. Drake had betrayed him. His parents had ridden him, never cutting him any slack. What was he supposed to do? He couldn't handle it. Was that such a sin?

Okay, I make mistakes, he thought as he lifted another big

can and struck it against the tailgate. I ran up against a part of life I couldn't handle. So I used something to get me over the hump.

He'd been so down. Finally, in desperation, he'd gone to his desk and dug out a little plastic bag Drake had given him to hold. In it were five pills. Drake said they were dynamite—that they'd make the world go away. His exact words. And that's exactly what David wanted.

But after a while the pills didn't do enough. He took more and more, and they were doing less and less. So he stepped up. A little weed with the pills. Or vodka. Then, at a party he'd done some crack. Big deal!

And that's exactly what the judge had said it was. A very big deal. He'd been busted for drunk driving. Luckily, he didn't have any drugs on him at the time. Unluckily, the cops called his old man, who came and got him.

Dad chewed him out all the way home. And his mom was crying in the kitchen. Shees! Why couldn't they understand he was hurting?

Because they didn't want to understand, he figured. They wanted to lay down laws and have their laws obeyed. That's what he told them too.

"You don't care about me. All you care about is what the neighbors might think if they knew you had a druggie living in your house!" he'd said.

"Is it such a crime to want to be respected, David?" his dad had replied.

"No! That's what I want! Why can't you respect me?" he'd screamed.

"Because you're a drunk and an addict!" his father shouted back. "What's to respect?"

"And you're a hypocrite!" David yelled, inches from his father's face. He backed up and raised his hands above his head. "I'm an addict! I'm an addict! John Pearce's son is a drug addict! What do you think of that, world?"

"Get out!"

It was the last thing he heard his father say. That was two weeks ago. He'd shown up at the trial, but hadn't said a word to his son. All through the trial David had wanted to say he was sorry. He'd been drunk when he said those things. He didn't mean them. But he didn't say it. And he didn't know why.

JUST THIS ONCE

"Hey, boy? You gonna look that trash into this truck?" Jones was talking. "Them cans ain't gonna jump up there on they own."

"Yeah, yeah." He could hear them laughing at him. Well go ahead and laugh, he thought. Two more weeks of this and I'm outa here.

He laughed to himself. Two weeks? Two hours! Two hours, and I go over to Wooster Place. There's supposed to be some new stuff coming in tonight. It's supposed to be the best. Make the world go away.

Blind choice:
Without looking ahead, turn to page 102 or page 129 to learn what happens to David.

JUST THIS ONCE 113

"I think we should stop talking and *do* something," David finally said. "Maybe we can't change the world, but at least we can make a difference."

That was all the group needed to get going. John Metzger agreed to find a faculty sponsor. Sammy Wu would do publicity. And David would organize the first meeting.

"We are, as of last Friday, an official, school-sponsored, student organization," David said two weeks later. "So I hereby call to order this meeting of Students Against Driving Drunk, hereafter called SADD." He felt a little self-conscious. He'd never intended to be president. He looked to Mr. Hamner for help. What next?

"I'm only the sponsor," Mr. Hamner said. "It's your group." David had never seen him like this. Relaxed. His tie loosened and the top button of his shirt undone.

"Well ... uh ... The stuff hasn't come from the national office yet ... So, in the meantime, I guess our first order of business is to figure out ways to keep kids from driving drunk." Everyone just looked at him.

Finally, John spoke up. "Maybe it would help if we listed the things teenagers do where they drink or use drugs."

"Well, graduation is one," Rachael Thomas suggested. "Seniors drink like fish at graduation time."

"And ball games," Trent Dressler said. "Especially the big ones and when we win. Like against Monroe in football."

"And private parties," Bobby Themes offered.

Sammy spoke up. "Come on, you guys. You haven't hit the big one yet ... The grand prize." Everyone looked at each other, puzzled.

"Come on!" Sammy encouraged them. Silence ... "Okay, I'll give you a hint. It involves dancing."

Rachael flew out of her chair. "Prom!" she shouted.

"You're right!" Bobby said, smiling at Sammy.

"Okay," David said, seeing his opportunity. "Let's focus on the prom. Suggestions?"

"A drug-and-alcohol-free prom," offered John.

"Dream on," Sammy said, rolling her eyes.

"No," Rachael said, sitting down. "It could work." She was obviously excited. "I'm on the prom committee. And, you know, we could make it something special, see. Not like we're taking something away, but like we're adding something." She was talking so fast it didn't make much sense.

"What could we add?" asked Trent.

"Well, like, transportation," she said. "That way no one would have to drive. We could raise the money and hire a fleet of limos to drive us."

"Rachael," John interrupted. "That would cost more money than the school district has, let alone student council."

"Okay, so we don't use limos. We use something else."

"Like what?"

"Like a bus," Mr. Hamner said. Everyone stopped talking and looked at him. It was the first thing he'd said since the meeting started. "Maybe we could get one of those fancy ones. Probably take a couple or three of them."

"You think?" David said.

"Sure," Mr. Hamner said, smiling. "I'd bet the P.T.A. might even kick in some money for something like this."

"Whoa!" John interjected.

"We could fix 'em up," Sammy said. "You know, decorate them inside."

■

So it happened. The planning of the first drug-and-alcohol-free Tecumseh High School Junior/Senior Prom.

And it worked. Beautifully. They chartered three busses, and the student council—which didn't like the idea at first but was finally persuaded—decorated them with crepe paper and balloons.

The bus ride was included in the price of a prom ticket, and everyone had to ride the bus to get in. Two sets of parents were on each bus serving hors d'oeuvres as they rode to the prom at the Sheldon Manor Hotel.

The after-prom party was scheduled at another location. Food, desserts and huge, frozen, alcohol-free fruit-punch cocktails were served by four fathers dressed as waiters.

Halfway through the party, David found himself dancing with Sammy Wu. He hadn't seen her all night, so he was anxious to get her impressions. It was a little hard to talk as they danced. But the DJ was playing a nice, slow blues number that only required swaying back and forth.

JUST THIS ONCE   **115**

"So, what d'ya think?" David asked.

She smiled. "I think it's great," she said.

"Some kids didn't come," he said, a little disappointment in his voice.

"But a whole lot of kids did," she answered. "We did a lot of good here, David ... Probably saved some lives."

David nodded and smiled. "Yeah," he said. "We probably did."

The End

David thought a long time about his choices and decided his parents were right. He'd be better off not drinking at all. He decided to talk about it during Sunday school.

"I've been doing some research. I looked it up," David said the next Sunday morning. He paged quickly through his Bible. "Here ... Proverbs 20:1. Drinking too much makes you loud and foolish. It's stupid to get drunk."

"Everybody knows that," Rachael Thomas said. "So what?"

David looked to Mr. Becker for help. Mr. Becker just raised his eyebrows and shrugged his shoulders. If he knew, he wasn't telling.

David looked back at the page. "Well," he said, hesitantly. "It seems like it's easy to get drunk before you know it's happening."

Sammy Wu shrugged her shoulders. "Yeah. But Jesus turned water into wine at a wedding because the host ran out. And it was good wine too."

"That's not the point ... "

"Yes it is. You can't say that the Bible is against drinking, because even Jesus drank wine. All those guys did. Moses, Paul, David ... everyone."

David sighed. He'd thought this would be easier. This was a Sunday school class. "But that's all they had back then. It was like ... like ... "

"Coke," Mr. Becker said quietly.

"Yeah, like Coke." David wasn't sure he was winning this argument. He wished Mr. Becker would help him out a little more.

"What does Paul say?" Mr. Becker asked.

"Well, not much," David said.

"Doesn't he? Try ... uh ... Romans." Mr. Becker thumbed through his Bible. "Here it is: Romans 12:1. Trent, you wanna read it for us?"

Trent jumped. "Uh, yeah, okay. Let's see, 'So then, my brothers, because of God's great mercy to us I appeal to you: Offer yourselves as a living sacrifice to God, dedicated to his service and pleasing to him.' "

"I think I get it!" Sammy said, closing her Bible. "I guess we're supposed to treat ourselves as if we were sacrifices to God. The very best, the finest."

"Kinda hard to do if your body's polluted," Rachael said.

"Yeah," David said. "So it's not drinking or drugs in particular that Paul's against. It's anything that hurts us."

Mr. Becker nodded. "The Bible tends to deal with morals more than with specific shoulds and shouldn'ts. We have to interpret it for our own lives."

"Sheesh!" John Metzger said. "That makes everything so hard. Why can't it just say do this, don't do that? Like the Ten Commandments."

"And how do you explain all this to other people?" Sammy asked the group. "People who aren't Christians? People who don't know about Paul—or even the Bible, for that matter?"

"Maybe you don't explain," Mr. Becker said. "Maybe you just don't drink. Maybe you live it instead of talking about it."

"Yeah, maybe," said David. "But I think we should talk about it too. And that's what I'm going to do starting tomorrow at school."

Blind choice:
Without looking ahead, turn to page 41 or page 79 to see how David's friends will respond.

JUST THIS ONCE

The harassment didn't start immediately. People waited till lunch.

Jabs from people David thought were his friends—people he'd counted on for support—hurt the worst. He could shrug off remarks from the druggies and troublemakers. But these were supposed to be his friends.

It started when he was paying for his meal.

"Hey, Dave, better watch it. That Coke's got caffeine in it. Wouldn't want to get any drugs in your system, would you?"

"Whoa! Is that a brownie on your tray, Davo? Doesn't sugar have a narcotic effect on some people?"

"Yeah, and chocolate has caffeine. Is our hero a *chocoholic?*"

By this time, David had made it to a long cafeteria table. Someone swiped the salt shaker out of his hand just as he picked it up. "Tsk, tsk. Sodium chloride, Dave. Can't be putting chemicals in our system, can we?"

They didn't mean to be mean. They were just kidding. They'd laugh and pat him on the back. "You gotta lighten up a little, Dave," Drake finally told him. "It's no worse here than anywhere else."

Mercifully, the lunch bell rang before the teasing became intolerable. As he sat in his government class, he tried to figure out what to do. He figured he had two options. He could rethink his position to ease the teasing. Or he could ignore the teasing and begin doing something about the problem.

What would you do?

If David reconsiders his position, turn to page 16.
If David decides to begin addressing the problem, turn to page 44.

"I guess there's not really anything we can do about it," David finally conceded.

The others agreed. The problem was too big for them. After all, Rachael noted, they were just high school kids.

David felt depressed, sad and powerless.

Finally he went to his pastor again. Jeff Marsh sympathized, but he didn't offer advice. That wasn't Jeff's way. He helped David figure out what he wanted to do—should do. But he never told him what to do. And they prayed together. Asking for God's guidance and help and courage.

Then David stumbled onto an idea. He called it The Covenant. Basically, it was an agreement a student would sign saying he or she would stay drug- and alcohol-free for the school year.

That was it. Simple.

David got his dad to help him write it with a lot of "whereases" and "therefore, be it resolveds." But it was really simple. He got a girl he knew in art class to make it look like an official document. And Jeff let him copy it on the church's big photocopier.

That had been the easy part. Now the hard part began—convincing people to sign and live by the agreement.

He didn't call the kids in the old SADD chapter. First he wanted to show that it could really be done. So he started with the football team, working like a high-pressure salesman.

First he asked. Then he pleaded, argued and badgered. Whatever it took: "If we get everyone in the school to sign, they'll stop the locker searches." "The team will be better." "Our parents will trust us more."

And, slowly, people began to sign. First Tom Fisher—one of Drake's friends. He said, "I guess I might as well be the first."

Then Brian Donnenworth. "Tom signed?" he queried. "No stuff? Well, okay. Gimme the pen."

Then others. And, finally, Bert Roberts, #12 to sign—half the team. The rest would be ... well, not easy. But easier now. With God's help, he told himself, the other players would sign. Then the cheerleaders and the band and ...

Well, one at a time.

He smiled as he saw Bobby walking down the hall. Time to recruit help.

The End

120　JUST THIS ONCE

Taking it real easy meant going real slow and watching the center line in the road. Everything else he tried to watch kept doubling and tripling before his eyes.

Once, about a mile from Drake's house, another car came down the road toward him, and he thought it was three cars lined up across the road. He swerved to get out of the way, and hit some trash cans.

Close call! Gotta keep this baby on the road. Just aim it down that center line, and follow the line home.

So that's what he did. He put everything he had into watching that center line. That's why he didn't see the stop sign. Or the station wagon coming across the intersection.

He hit it going 30 miles per hour, pushing it across the intersection and up against a tree in someone's yard. Later, he learned that the driver—a teacher from Monroe—had a concussion and a broken arm. His wife had a big cut on her head where she hit the windshield.

The little girl who'd been asleep in the back seat was still unconscious when David's parents arrived in the emergency room. They found him slumped in a chair, holding a cold compress to his broken nose. In his shirt pocket was the police citation: "Driving Under the Influence."

Blind choice:
Without looking ahead, turn to page 74 or page 109 to discover David's parents' reaction.

He couldn't risk losing Rita this way. Later he could turn her down when he knew she wouldn't leave because of it.

"Sure," he said awkwardly as he pulled into a parking lot.

Rita reached down to turn up the radio and, in the same motion, engaged the car's cigarette lighter. In a couple of seconds it popped out. She lit the joint and sucked the smoke deep into her lungs.

She blew it out, leaned the seat back and passed the joint to David.

His hand shook nervously as he took the weed. He put it to his lips, sucked in and tasted the sweet smoke as it went into his lungs. At first he wanted to cough and choke. But after a few seconds, the hit began to relax him. It felt soothing after the hard game.

They sat together in silence, his arm around her, and passed the joint back and forth.

After taking the last hit, Rita asked, "Wanna get some munchies?"

"Okay," David said. "What, hamburgers?"

"Nah, let's get some stuff and go up to Stanley."

David's heart almost stopped. Stanley Memorial Park was a notorious necking spot just outside the city limits. This must be his lucky night.

He drove to a 7-11 and bought diet Coke and a bag of munchies while Rita sat in the car. When he got back, she'd stacked the coats on the console. She leaned over, putting her hand on his leg and leaning her head on his shoulder.

David made it to Stanley in record time.

■

The diet Coke and munchies were forgotten.

David and Rita started kissing in the car, but the stupid console and the steering wheel kept getting in the way. So David got the big, scratchy army blanket out of the trunk, and they lay on it in the grass.

It was cool outside the car, but it was nice. Very nice, he decided. They were enveloped by the night and they folded one end of the blanket over them for warmth. Their kissing was a little hesitant at first, but gradually they gained confidence and their passion grew.

JUST THIS ONCE

His breathing was heavy now as she whispered her love for him. And they kissed, deeper and more passionately each time.

This was exciting and wonderful and ... and kind of scary, David thought. Three hours ago, he'd hardly had the courage even to ask her out. And now ... It was all moving so fast. Maybe *too* fast!

The weed was making it hard for David to think clearly. He knew he should stop. But could he? Would he? He might not ever have another opportunity like this with Rita.

What would you do?
If David interrupts the passion, turn to page 49.
If David decides to keep going, turn to page 127.

"No one ever said the right thing is the easy thing," Mr. Pearce said, as he poured coffee into his cup. He offered David the pot.

David poured some into his own mug. "But they blame me!" he said.

"They're mad and frustrated, David," his mother said. "They need someone to blame. And you're just an easy target."

David sipped his coffee and looked around the kitchen. It was a little after 11 p.m. The house was quiet except for the clock ticking in the living room. It was easy to be against drugs and alcohol here ... where it was safe.

"I just don't understand it. Kids who never did dope in their lives—who'd never take a drink. Even they were mad at me," he said.

His father nodded. "Jeff Marsh talked about this same kind of thing in his sermon a couple of weeks ago."

"Yes," Mrs. Pearce jumped in. "Something from one of Paul's letters." She grabbed a Bible from the buffet and found an old worship bulletin tucked in the front cover. "Here it is: 2 Timothy 4:7. 'I have done my best in the race, I have run the full distance, and I have kept the faith.'"

Mr. Pearce was still nodding his head. "The point is, David, God doesn't expect us to win every race we enter. But he does expect us to complete the task. To be faithful. To stand by what we believe."

Mrs. Pearce stirred her coffee. "I think what you're doing is wonderful, son. It takes guts to stand up for what you believe when everyone else seems to be against you."

David was a little embarrassed by all of this praise. "Oh, Mom, they're not *all* against me. There are lots of kids who think drugs and alcohol are stupid. But they're quiet about it. They do what they believe in, but they don't force their beliefs on other people."

"You mean they don't talk about what they believe? I don't remember you putting a gun to anyone's head and saying 'Don't do drugs, or I'll blow your brains out,'" Mr. Pearce said.

David smiled. "No, they're blowing their own brains out already."

"Well, there you go, then. You're not forcing anything on anyone. You're doing what God expects us all to do. You're being a Christian, and you're not being ashamed of it."

David shrugged. "I guess ... I just wish there was an easier way."

"No one likes being ridiculed, David," Mrs. Pearce said. "Not even Jesus. But he put up with it, because the cause was important."

David had to agree. If the commitment to the cause was strong enough, you could do anything. Look at John Brown and the slave revolts. Or Martin Luther King Jr. Or the "righteous Gentiles" he had read about in history class—the ones who had risked their lives and their families to save their Jewish friends and neighbors during World War II.

But he didn't have to go that far. Look at his own parents. Had they ever thought about how much they'd given up for him? If they had, he'd never heard them. They just did it. Because the commitment was strong.

That night, as he lay in bed staring at the plaster swirls in the ceiling, David decided. He would have a cause. Like Dr. King and John Brown and the righteous Gentiles. Only his cause would be sobriety.

■

David decided to take his cause to junior high kids—before it was too late for them. He was a teen counselor—one of the senior high kids who went over to the junior high once a week at lunch hour to help the younger kids with homework or whatever.

It took him two weeks to prepare his presentation, using information from the local police department, the Eastside Clinic and Students Against Driving Drunk. But he put all the information together and wrote his speech.

On the last school day before finals, he gave a special program. He showed slides of drugs and drug paraphernalia. He told stories about what drugs had done to people he'd met at the clinic. Then he closed his speech: "Drugs and alcohol are poisons. That's why your body reacts to them the way it does. It's trying to tell you that what you're doing to it is destructive. It's saying, 'Stop! You're hurting me!'

"Some of us listen to our bodies. We hear the message, and we quit. But others—the ones who don't quit? They die. Maybe not today or tomorrow. But eventually. They poison their minds, their bodies, their spirits and ... eventually, the poison kills them.

"'Just Say No' isn't enough. It should be 'Must Say No!' We *must* say no to drugs and alcohol. They'll kill us if we don't."

He didn't get a standing ovation. Not even a big round of applause. But he did see one kid. A little seventh-grade guy nodding his head near the middle of the crowd.

One little kid. Not much. But it was all David needed. He was running the race. He was fighting the good fight.

The End

"Mr. Pearce?"

The cop was looking at David's driver's license with a long, black flashlight. "Mr. Pearce," he said again, looking up at David. "You have failed the standard test for blood alcohol content. Your blood alcohol content is of a sufficient level to consider you intoxicated. Do you understand?"

David nodded. Why was he talking so loud?

"Mr. Pearce, you'll have to come with us. We'll send a wrecker for your car. You are under arrest. You have the right to remain silent. Anything you say can and will be used against you in a court of law. Understand?"

"Uh, yeah." A wrecker? He hadn't had a wreck. What was the problem? Weaving! The cop said he was weaving. But how could he have been ...

"... if you can't afford a lawyer, one will be appointed to you by the court. Do you understand your rights as I have read them to you?"

"Yeah ... uh ... my parents ... "

"We'll call them from the station," the cop said. He put his hand on top of David's head and pushed him into the back seat of the police cruiser. "Try not to puke on the seats, okay?"

"Yeah," David said. But he didn't know if he could keep his word. His parents. Oh, dear Lord. What would they say to him? What would they do?

Blind choice:

Without looking ahead, turn to page 74 or page 109 to learn how David's parents respond.

As they kissed again, her hand moved up behind his head and her fingers played in his hair. And he decided he didn't care. Weed, love—what was the difference? Who cared?

Making love to his dream girl on a warm blanket in Stanley Memorial Park. He couldn't believe it was happening. Stop thinking, he told himself. Just go with it.

Later, he lay on his back looking at the stars. Rita lay snuggled up to him on her side, her arm on his chest, his right arm under her head. Her breathing was deep and regular, like she was asleep. He didn't know for sure.

And he didn't want to know. If she was awake he would have to say something, and he didn't know what to say. He knew eventually they'd have to get up and go home. But he was putting it off.

Why did he feel so awful? So guilty? Isn't this what he'd wanted?

No, he guessed it wasn't. Not this way. Something was wrong. Something? Everything! Why had he let himself go all the way? He knew it was wrong. Why hadn't he stopped?

Rita snuggled closer and kissed his cheek. He turned his head to kiss her and, immediately, he knew the other problem. He smelled it: the weed.

Had she really meant what she said? Did she really love him? Or was it the drug talking? Had she really been all that willing? Or had he taken advantage of her because she was high? He wished he knew.

"Rita?" he said, jostling her.

"M-m-m."

"We'd better go," he said, sitting up on the blanket.

She sat up and began straightening her clothes. "Okay," she said.

David could tell she hadn't been asleep. She had been stalling too. He felt like he should say something, but he didn't know what. I'm sorry? Are you okay? No, the words sounded stupid.

They drove home in silence. Rita leaned against him, clinging to his arm. But it wasn't the same. He felt like she was just doing it because it was the thing to do—after what had happened and all.

JUST THIS ONCE

I wonder if she's pregnant, he thought as he drove. He could feel the panic building in his chest. No! Stop! Take it one step at a time. Talk to her.

But he couldn't. He couldn't think of anything to say.

Maybe he should talk to Drake, he thought. Drake, his best friend, was more familiar with this kind of thing—at least he said he was. But how could he talk to Drake without sounding like "locker room" talk?

After a long goodnight kiss, he said goodbye to Rita at her front door and went home.

David tried to sleep, but the evening—and his questions—kept his mind racing. Maybe he should just call Drake. Or would it be better to wait to talk to Rita?

What would you do?

If he talks to Rita, turn to page 59.
If he calls Drake for advice, turn to page 30.

Just off Wooster Place, 3645 Devo Street was a crack house. Anyone who thought about it knew it. But no one thought about it very much.

Thinking about it could get you killed. Killed by crack dealers who didn't care about anything except the $50,000 or $60,000 they could make a week dealing crack. So you kept your mouth shut, looked the other way and walked by on the other side of the street ... if you dared walk down it at all.

All that was true unless you were going to 3645 Devo Street.

So "Dave the Dude" Pearce walked right down the sidewalk on the same side of the street as the house. He didn't think of the danger. He didn't think of the problems that might face him. All he thought about was the vial of crack waiting for him in that house.

There was other stuff in the house if you wanted it. There were girls who'd have sex with you for a $5 vial. And guys, too, for that matter. And there were watches and guns and knives and televisions and all kinds of stuff people had tried to trade for crack and left lying around when they were told to come back with some long green.

But no one going to a crack house was interested in having sex or shooting a gun or watching television. They were just interested in smoking crack and getting high and smoking more crack until the money ran out.

That's what David was going to do. He'd just made a big score on a stereo and television he'd lifted from a house up near where he used to live. And he'd gotten $50 from a fence.

He cut across a bare yard and went up to the porch where a big guy with a bulge in his windbreaker, near his arm pit, grabbed him and slammed him up against the wall.

"Spread 'em," the guy said. "Just like for the cops." He patted David down for weapons. "You got nickels and dimes?"

David showed him the $50.

"Go on in. Have a nice day," the guy said, smiling.

The minute he got inside the house it hit him. His nose started running, his legs got weak, he felt nauseated and dizzy. He needed a hit, bad.

It was a slow night. He only had to step over six people lying around on the floor. Some were passed out. Some were just high, nodding to the sound of the music that was playing on a big boom box in the corner. David saw that his spot was empty. The place he liked to nod out was over by the window, under the shredded curtains. Get the crack first, he said to himself.

He made his way to the door that led into what must have been the kitchen or maybe the dining room. Now it was nailed shut and there was a rectangular hole cut in it about waist high. He shoved $30 into the hole and waited. Might as well save the $20 for a while. He'd probably smoke it too, but you never knew. Right now he didn't want to think about later. He wanted to think about smoke. Yes, why was it taking them so long?

He thought about pounding on the door. But before he could, a plastic sandwich bag flew out of the hole and landed at his feet. He snatched it up quickly and looked around the room. Five of the six people in the room had seen it and were watching him.

Well, he'd watch them too. You couldn't be too careful. You get high, and these animals will steal your dope. That's why he liked his place. There was a little hole by the baseboard there that you could slip your dope into while you smoked.

He sat down and prepared his pipe. Set the crack in the little bowl and lit it with a Bic lighter. Inhaled it deeply into his lungs.

Something was wrong! Crack always burned, but this was more than a burn ... it hurt. It was like a sledgehammer had hit him in the chest.

He sucked on the pipe again. Something. Anything to make this pain go away. But it only got worse. His hand spasmed, and the glass pipe broke. Blood began to trickle down his arm.

Another sledgehammer blow. He screamed. Got to his hands and knees, tried to stand, but fell back down again.

"Help me!" he shouted. But it didn't come out like a shout. More like a little yelp. Now his chest was being crushed in a huge vice, and the pain began to crawl up his neck and down into his groin. "Help me! Please!"

He collapsed on the floor, his face falling into the glass of his broken pipe. But he didn't feel it. He felt nothing but the crushing, pounding, agonizing pain radiating through his torso.

■

Swami and Jungle Muffin watched the guy across the room twitch and thrash around and open his mouth like he was going to scream. But only a little yelp came out. Finally the guy just lay there, his face and hand bleeding from where he'd cut them on the broken pipe.

Jungle Muffin looked around the room. The other people were just sitting there—too high to know or care what was going on. She looked at Swami, and he shrugged.

She crawled across the room and knew Swami would follow. He always did. She reached the guy in the school jacket and reached over to touch his neck.

"Is he ..." Swami said.

She nodded. "Keep your voice down. He's dead."

"Crack git 'im?"

"Nah. Had a heart attack. Din't you see?"

"That what that was?" Swami asked, unbelieving.

"Sure. Happ'ns all the time."

"He must be old."

"Nah, he ain't no older'n you or me. Maybe 17 or 18. He just looks old. Crack does that. Look in a mirror sometime."

But Swami wasn't listening. "Hey, Muff, he keep his stash behind his back." He began to probe at the baseboard under the window and the board fell away. "See!" he said, holding up the bag of crack vials.

"All right, Swami! My man."

Swami beamed. "You wanna?" Swami began to crawl back to their place on the opposite wall, but Jungle Muffin stopped and turned back. She reached into David's pants pockets.

Wallet. No cards or money. She tossed it aside. Nothing else ... no, wait. What's this? She pulled out the $20 bill and held it up for Swami. He raised his fist and nodded his head in approval.

The End

David walked home from church. He needed to think. It was clear he needed help. He was in way over his head. But who could he ask? He sat on a bus-stop bench to think.

Coach Clark? No way. That would just get Drake kicked off the team. Coach was a stickler for rules.

Mr. Hamner, the vice principal? Maybe. He didn't know Mr. Hamner very well. Some of the kids called him Hamner the Hammer. But he seemed okay.

"We missed you at Home Boy's, David," Rachael said, stepping up beside him and catching him totally off guard. He didn't realize he'd been sitting there so long. "Blueberry pancakes will be the death of me." She smiled. "What's the matter? You look down."

Before he could answer, John stepped up on his other side. "Say, Dave. Didn't see you at Home Boy's."

"Sorry." David suspected John really wanted to talk to Rachael. Everyone knew he liked her. But she never seemed to notice.

She pointed at David, "Doesn't he look down to you, John?"

John shrugged. "Maybe. What's up—or down, as the case may be?"

David got up and started walking with his friends. He didn't know what to say. Would he be breaking Drake's confidence by telling his friends about the conversation? But how could he help Drake if he didn't talk to someone?

Finally, he decided to tell them. He told the whole story—about the night before, about the parking lot. He didn't leave anything out.

"Whew," John said, shaking his head when David was finished. "That's down, all right. What'cha gonna do?"

"He's gonna help, of course," Rachael said, indignantly.

"Help who? You, Rachael? You don't need help. John would be glad to help you, I'm sure." It was Samantha Wu. They'd just turned the corner in front of her house and hadn't noticed her raking leaves in her yard. She was a cute, smart sophomore. Everyone called her Sammy. It fit her personality.

"Thanks, Sammy," John said, embarrassed.

"We're talking about Drake Underwood," said Rachael, impatiently.

"What about him?" asked Sammy. "He's an alcoholic."

Everyone was shocked into silence. David didn't see his friend that way. An alcoholic? No, he just had some trouble with his drinking. He wasn't some slobbering, old wino in a gutter downtown.

"Well, isn't he?" Sammy asked as though it was a natural question.

"Well, I ... I don't know ... I mean, he ...," David stuttered.

"Oh, gimme a break," Sammy said, dropping her rake in the big pile of leaves she'd been collecting. "Does he drink?"

"Uh, yeah."

"A lot?"

David nodded.

"And his drinking is causing problems in his life, right?"

No need to answer. They all knew it was.

"But he keeps drinking anyway, doesn't he?" Sammy asked.

"Yeah," David said, seeing the whole thing coming together. "He does."

"Well," Sammy said, taking off her gloves and knocking the dust out of them on her leg. "Then he's an alcoholic. My dad says that's the test."

Now David remembered. Her dad was a psychologist.

"Has he tried to quit?"

"Thousands of times. He can't."

"Makes sense. Less than 10 percent of recovering alcoholics have managed to quit drinking on their own. They need help."

Rachael sighed. "That's what we're talking about, Sammy—how we can help Drake."

"How about your dad, Sam?" asked John.

"No," she said, shaking her head, serious now. "Not his field. How about Rev. Marsh? Didn't he used to do some drug counseling or something?"

"He volunteered at a clinic," said Rachael. "That doesn't qualify him."

"No," David said. "But he probably knows where to find someone who's qualified."

"Maybe," Rachael allowed. "You think he's still at the church?"

"I'll call and see," said Sammy, running toward the house.

The pastor had gone home, but he agreed to meet the teenagers at the church. They walked back to the church to talk. Hearing their story and their concern, he called psychologist Dr. Eric

Frieze, who worked at a mental health clinic on the east side of town. Dr. Frieze agreed to meet with the teenagers that Monday evening.

■

When David and the others arrived for the meeting, they recognized Dr. Frieze even though they'd never seen him. He looked exactly like a psychologist—beard, tweed jacket and wool tie.

The teenagers explained their perceptions and concerns about Drake. The psychologist listened and agreed that Drake had a serious problem.

"It sounds like Drake needs help," he explained. "And the only way to give it to him is to get him to confront his problem."

"But I've tried that," David protested. "It doesn't work."

"We need to arrange an intervention—a meeting of all the important people in Drake's life."

He asked for names, and the teenagers suggested several. Drake's parents. David's parents. Other friends. Coach Clark.

"I need you guys to call all these people and ask them to come to a meeting next Sunday evening. Then we'll get Drake to the meeting."

"But I can't betray Drake!" David argued. "He told me that stuff as a friend. He'll never forgive me if I tell all those people—and then trick him into coming to the meeting."

"Doing nothing is the worst kind of betrayal," Dr. Frieze explained. "Alcohol is a poison. Drake is killing himself. If he was holding a gun to his head you'd do whatever it took. Think of it that way. Those beers he keeps in the trunk of his car are all like loaded guns."

All four teenagers agreed to help organize the meeting. It wasn't easy, but they got everyone to agree to come. They also agreed to meet with Dr. Frieze during the week to talk about how the intervention would work.

Drake was the hardest. Finally, they decided David would pick him up and say he wanted to talk about some stuff.

■

The plan worked. Drake was clean, sober and reasonably well-rested when he walked into the room. Shock, surprise, wonder, doubt, worry and anxiety all flashed across his face when he

JUST THIS ONCE **135**

saw his friends, parents and coach seated in a circle in the middle of the youth room.

"Drake, I'm Dr. Frieze from Eastside Clinic. I asked your friends to call these folks here tonight. They have some things they'd like to tell you."

And the intervention began. First, people in the circle each told Drake about a time when his drinking had hurt or embarrassed them. They told about what they saw alcohol doing to him.

Then they told him what they wanted him to do. Enter the clinic as a patient. Tonight. Go with Dr. Frieze and start getting well.

If he didn't? That was the hard part. They would drop him. No invitations. No friends. No lying to protect him. No making excuses for him. He would no longer be part of their group. He would have to move out of his home. He would be on his own.

They didn't stop there. One by one, each person said: "I love you, Drake. I want you to be well. I won't watch you kill yourself with alcohol."

Then it was over. It was up to Drake now. Dr. Frieze had said this would be the hardest part—wanting so desperately to go to him, to hug him, and not being able to do it. They had to let him—make him—make his own decision to get well.

David wiped a tear from his eye, and Sammy handed him a tissue. It was soggy from her own tears.

Why didn't Drake say something? Why did he just sit there with his head down and his elbows on his knees? What was he thinking?

Finally, Drake raised his head and looked around the room.

Blind choice:
Without looking ahead, turn to page 20 or page 88 to discover Drake's reaction.

"When we started, we only had six kids in the group," David said. He was nervous talking to a group this big. "And our motives were mixed."

"I just wanted the locker searches to stop," Sammy explained.

"Did they?" A tall, serious-looking kid from Baylor High asked.

"Not at first," Sammy responded. "But later, they realized we were serious and were making a difference. So they eased up."

It was a bigger group than David had expected. Mr. Hamner had said a few kids from other schools wanted to hear about the famous Tecumseh High School drug program. David didn't even think of their group as a drug "program." It was just he and some of his friends trying to do something.

But 50 or 60 students from Baylor High, Brindelton, Jackson, Monroe and a couple of private schools must've been impressed. They were crowded into the media center drinking fruit punch, eating chocolate chip cookies and wanting to know how Tecumseh High had managed such a decisive victory in the war on drugs.

"When did the administration realize ... I mean ... when did you realize that you were making a difference?" someone asked.

Bobby Themes fielded this one. "Well," he said in that measured, unhurried way he was known for. "It didn't come quickly, I can tell you. It seemed like we worked and worked for months with no results."

Sammy couldn't stand it. Bobby was just too slow. "Then, all of a sudden things started to pop," she interrupted. "The first thing was the Contract for Life. We had about 50 kids sign it."

"Only 50?" asked a girl with the Brindelton group.

"Well, kids don't like to talk about drugs and stuff with their parents," Sammy explained. "And a lot of parents don't want to admit that their kids might need their help because of drugs or alcohol."

"So," Rachael chimed in. "We drew up the Contract for Life. You have copies of it in the packet we gave you. It's just a simple document that kids sign that says they'll stay drug- and alcohol-free for the school year."

"What about next year?" a teacher from one of the schools asked.

"Next year we ask them to sign a new contract," John said.

"The important thing is, we've gotten 200 kids to sign it already. That's a third of the student body."

"Another breakthrough was the program at the junior high." Several faces were blank. They hadn't heard about the peer counseling program.

David explained. "A group of us had been going to the junior high every Tuesday and Thursday to tutor. We just asked if we could do a kind of peer counseling thing too. We'd be someone older—but not an adult—who younger kids could talk to. We thought we could deal with the problems of drug and alcohol abuse as we talked about other stuff."

A tall girl in the middle shook her head and said, "My brother's in the seventh grade, and I'd pay money *not* to have to talk to him!"

"The big thing, though, was the prom," Rachael said, as the laughter quieted. "The drug-and-alcohol-free prom was what won us the respect of the school administration and the Parent-Teacher Association."

"It was great," Sammy added. "We worked it out so everyone could have a great time without drinking. No driving. No being out of touch. No private parties. We just partied all night together."

"First, everyone rode busses to the prom. Then the prom," Trent explained. "Then after the dance, we had an all-night party with a band, food and alcohol-free drinks. We attracted people with games and prizes. And parents dressed up and served us."

"You had parents at your prom?" an incredulous person asked.

"Well," David explained. "Not just any parents. They had to apply."

The room broke up into laughter again. "No, really," David insisted. "Each parent who wanted to be a chaperone had to fill out a questionnaire and an application. Then we chose 10 parents we wanted to be our servers and chaperones. Copies of the application form are in your packets."

No one in the room seemed to believe their approach. David shrugged. He hadn't really believed it at first either. But it worked well. He'd been amazed when the prom committee chose his own parents to be chaperones.

And he had been even more amazed when his parents hadn't embarrassed him in some way. They were great, serving drinks and food and asking, "Will that be all, sir?" and winking at David. "We need to wrap it up," a teacher announced. "David, perhaps you could give us some last bit of wisdom to take with us."

David looked around at his group. Everyone smiled at him, but no one offered to help. He thought for a moment, stood and cleared his throat. "Well," he said and cleared his throat again. "I guess the biggest thing—the most important thing—is to not give up. If you're going to do any good, you have to really believe you can make a difference."

He looked back at his friends, still smiling. Okay, he said in a silent prayer, I believe. Thank you, God.

The End

"I really think we can help with this drug and alcohol problem," David said finally.

"Sure we can," Sammy Wu said sarcastically. "We can help old Hamner search kids' lockers. Wouldn't that make us popular?"

"I don't like the searches any more than you do, Sammy," David interrupted. "Hamner doesn't either. He wishes it was like it used to be when teachers could just teach and didn't have to be cops and social workers and babysitters and everything else."

"Then why doesn't he stop the searches?" John Metzger asked, though it didn't sound like he really cared. He was just interested.

"Well," David started, then stopped. He'd never been in the position of defending a vice principal before. It felt awkward. But he wasn't defending Hamner the Hammer as much as he was trying to explain him. "Well," he began again, "he feels like his back is to the wall. He sees these searches as the only way to beat the drug problem—to get the stuff out of the school."

Rachael Thomas picked up a piece of pizza, looked at it and set it back in the box. "Well, getting it out of the school doesn't solve the problem."

"Right," David said. "Are you going to eat that?"

Rachael shook her head and stuck out her tongue. "It's cold."

"Just like I like it," John said, snatching it before David could.

David tried to ignore it. "I think that's the whole problem."

Bobby Themes looked up. "What's the problem? Pizza?"

"No," David said, picking at some cheese stuck in the box. "The problem is that we're trying to solve the problem."

"Well, isn't that what we're here for?" Sammy asked.

David nodded. "Well, sorta. But maybe we're trying to tackle too much by trying to change everything and everyone." He paused to think. "I mean, we're just a few people. We can't solve the whole drug problem ourselves."

Rachael folded her arms. "What are we wasting time for?"

The light came on above Bobby's head. "No!" Bobby said, sitting up straight. "That's not what he's saying."

John popped the last bit of pizza into his mouth. "We need to lower our sights," Bobby said. "We need to set a realistic goal."

"Right," said David. "We can't change everyone's behavior. And we can't solve all the substance-abuse problems in the school."

Rachael sighed. "Then what are we ..."

David cut her off. "But we can offer one answer—something for people who want an alternative."

"For instance?" Sammy asked.

David pulled a piece of paper out of his backpack. He moved the pizza box and laid the paper on the table. "Like this," he said.

Bobby began to read aloud. "Contract for Life. A contract for life between parent and teenager."

"We can read, Bobby," Sammy said.

He stuck out his tongue at her, and they all read in silence.

John responded first. "So if I drink too much or the person driving drinks too much, my folks agree to pick me up any time, day or night."

"Or send a cab or some kind of transportation," Sammy added.

"And they also agree not to drive drunk or ride with a drunk driver," David added. "And you agree to call them if you're in trouble."

"My mom would have a cow if I called her and told her I was too drunk to drive," Rachael said.

Bobby pointed to the paper. "Uh-uh. Not right then, anyway. It says so here. She agrees not to yell at you then, but to discuss it with you later."

"Well, what do you think?" David asked.

They all considered for a moment, looking at each other. Finally Sammy spoke. "You got any more of these?"

David reached into his backpack and pulled out at least a dozen contracts fanned out like a rummy hand. "I kinda thought you'd like it," he said. Immediately, each person drew a contract from his hands like they were playing Old Maid.

Rachael looked at her copy, then abruptly took a pen from John's pocket and signed the bottom. "There," she said, underlining Thomas with a flourish.

David was bursting with excitement inside. Maybe now they could make a difference at Tecumseh High. Maybe this was the first step.

Blind choice:

Without looking ahead, turn to page 81 or page 137 to see if the group makes a difference.

142 JUST THIS ONCE

David stormed out of the kitchen, leaving the bag of Oreos on the counter. He couldn't believe his mom would accuse Uncle John of alcoholism. They must've been jealous of how much fun Uncle John had.

David felt penned in, almost claustrophobic. Since his dad hadn't actually taken his keys yet, David figured he could still drive. So he grabbed his wallet and headed out.

■

To relax a little, David picked up a six-pack of beer at a convenience store that never checked I.D.s. Then he drove around a while, listening to the heavy metal station and sipping beer.

David wasn't sure how long he drove. All he knew was that it was getting dark. And it was getting harder to concentrate on the road. So he put all his energy into watching the center line. That's why he didn't see the stop sign. Or the station wagon coming across the intersection.

He hit it going 30 mph, pushing it across the intersection and up against a tree in someone's yard. Later, he learned that the driver—a teacher from Monroe—had a concussion and a broken arm.

When David's parents arrived in the emergency room, they found him slumped in a chair, holding a cold compress to his broken nose. In his shirt pocket was the police citation: "Driving Under the Influence."

Blind choice:
Without looking ahead, turn to page 74 or page 109 to discover David's parents' reaction.

What Would You Do?

*T*hree more **What Would You Do?** novels are now available ... filled with new characters, more spine-tingling decisions and loads of thrilling endings. Don't miss these three **What Would You Do?** novels ...

A Time to Belong—Help Ann make good decisions about friends.
ISBN 1-55945-051-7 $6.95

He Gave Her Roses—Give Stacy guidance with dating decisions.
ISBN 0-931529-92-1 $6.95

The Option Play—Control the decisions Matt makes as he experiences the thrills and pressures of high school sports.
ISBN 1-55945-050-9 $6.95

These and other Teenage Books *are available at your local Christian bookstore.* Or order direct from the publisher. Write Teenage Books, Box 481, Loveland, CO 80539. Please add $3 postage and handling per order. Colorado residents add 3% sales tax.